Knee High Nature
Winter

Knee High Nature
Winter

A Guide to Nature, Activities and Fun

*Dianne Hayley
& Pat Wishart*

*Illustrated
by Jo-El Berg*

LONE
PINE

First printed 1993 5 4 3 2 1
Portions originally published as *Knee High Nature: Winter in Alberta* 1988, fourth printing 1991
Printed in Canada

Printed on recycled paper

Canadian Cataloguing in Publication Data

Hayley, Dianne, 1944-
   Knee high nature : winter

Includes bibliographical references.
ISBN 1-51105-038-2 : 14.95

   1. Natural history—Canada, Northern—Juvenile literature. 2. Nature study—Canada, Northern—Juvenile literature. 3. Winter—Canada, Northern—Juvenile literature. 4. Natural history—Canada, Western—Juvenile literature. 5. Nature study—Canada, Western—Juvenile literature. 6. Winter—Canada, Western—Juvenile literature. 7. Natural history—Northwestern States—Juvenile literature. 8. Nature study—Northwestern States—Juvenile literature. 9. Winter—Northwestern States—Juvenile literature. I. Wishart, Pat. II. Berg, Jo-El. III. Title.
QH106.H39 1993   j574.971   C94-910048-X

 Knee High Nature gratefully acknowledges the financial assistance of Recreation, Parks and Wildlife Foundation and the Government of Canada, Science Culture Canada program in the production of this book.

The Publisher

Lone Pine Publishing
206, 10426 – 81 Avenue
Edmonton, Alberta, Canada T6E 1X5

Lone Pine Publishing
202A – 1110 Seymour Street
Vancouver, British Columbia, Canada V6B 3N3

Editorial and production: *Glenn Rollans*
Design, cover and layout: *Bruce Timothy Keith*
Front and back cover illustrations: *Jo-El Berg*
Printing: *Jasper Printing Group, Edmonton, Canada*

The publisher gratefully acknowledges the assistance of Heritage Canada, Alberta Community Development, and the financial support provided by the Alberta Foundation for the Arts in the production of this book.

ACKNOWLEDGMENTS

The authors gratefully acknowledge the very special help of the following people:

    Bill Wishart for his wildlife expertise in editing the text and for helping to
        keep us accurate.

    Don Hayley for his help with our computers.

    Joanne O'Hare for her contribution to the coyotes section.

We don't pretend to be experts in all fields, but we've called on experts for help and advice. Our thanks go to:

    The staff of Alberta Fish and Wildlife Services, in particular Arlen Todd ,
        John Gunson and Margo Pybus.

    The staff of Alberta Agriculture.

    The staff of Canadian Wildlife Service, in particular Lou Carbyn
        and Len Shandruk.

    The staff of John Janzen Nature Centre, in particular Sue Fast, Will Husby, Wendy Zelt
        and Grant Symons.

    The staff of the Strathcona Wilderness Centre.

    Naturalist and wildlife artist Deirdre Griffiths.

    Max Scharfenberger of the Edmonton Space & Science Centre.

    Sheila Abercrombie, Carol Carbyn, Ricki Romito, Mary Jefferies, Susan and Ben Mandrusiak,
        Robin Bovey, Bonnie Hamelin, Bill Abercrombie, Mary Pease, Jean Horne, Elspeth Berg, Debby
        Waldman and Barbara Demers for their helpful suggestions.

Our special thanks go to our families for their encouragement and support.

The following have granted us copyright permission to use their original works
in our book:

"Legend of the Pack Rat" by Kerry Wood. Published in *Birds and Animals in the Rockies*, Banff, Jasper. H.R. Larson Publishing Co., Saskatoon, Saskatchewan.

"My Mother Took Me Skating" from *It's Snowing, It's Snowing* by Jack Prelutsky. Copyright 1984. Reproduced by permission of Greenwillow Books. New York.

"Chickadees" by Harriet Jenks from: *The New High Road of Song for Nursery Schools and Kindergarten* by Fletcher and Denison. Copyright 1960. Canada Publishing Co., Toronto. Reprinted by permission of Gage Educational Publishing Co. Agincourt, Ontario.

"Mice" from *Fifty-One New Nursery Rhymes* by Rose Fyleman. Copyright 1931. Reproduced by permission of The Society of Authors as literary representative of the estate of Rose Fyleman. London, England.

"Morris Mouse and His Christmas Trees" from *Paper Stories* by Jean Stangl. Copyright 1984. David S. Lake Publishers, Belmont, California.

"The Mouse" from *The Handbook for Storytellers* by Caroline Feller Bauer. Copyright 1971. Chicago. With permission of the American Library Association.

"Santa Claus and the Mouse" from *Children's Counting-Out Rhymes, Fingerplays, Jump-Rope and Bounce-Ball Chants and Other Rhymes,* Copyright 1983 by Gloria T. Delamar by permission of McFarland & Company, Inc., Publishers, Jefferson NC.

"Raven and the Children" from *Raven, Creator of the World*, Eskimo Legends retold by Ronald Melzack. Copyright 1970. Reprinted by permission of the author.

"How the Fawn Got Its Spots" from *Keepers of the Animals*: *Native American Stories and Wildlife Activities for Children* by Michael J. Caduto and Joseph Bruchac. Copyright 1991. Fulcrum Publishing, 350 Indiana Street, Golden, Colorado 80401, USA.

The game "Oh Deer", adapted from *Project WILD Elementary Activity Guide*. Ottawa: Canadian Wildlife Federation, 1985. Permission from the Canadian Wildlife Federation.

Lyrics to "Rudolph, the Red-Nosed Reindeer" by Johnny Marks. Reprinted by permission of St. Nicholas Music Inc. Copyright 1949. Renewed 1977. All rights reserved. New York.

"Snowshoe Hare" from *Rabbits, Rabbits* by Aileen Fisher. Copyright © 1983 by Aileen Fisher. Reprinted by permission of Harper & Row, Publishers, Inc. New York.

"Little Brother Rabbit" from *Thirty Indian Legends of Canada*. Copyright © 1973 by Margaret Bemister. A Douglas & McIntyre Book.

"How Coyote Stole Fire" by Gail Robertson and Douglas Hill from *Coyote the Trickster* © 1975. Reprinted by permission of the authors' agents: Watson, Little Limited, London, England.

"Sly is the Word" from *The Fox Book* ed. Richard Shaw. Copyright 1971 by Frederick Warne & Co., Inc. All rights reserved. Reprinted by permission of Viking Penguin. Inc. New York.

"Coyotes" by Jon Whyte. Published in *Prairie Jungle*, ed. Wenda McArthur and Geoffrey Ursell. 1985. Coteau books, Thunder Creek Publishing Co-op. Moose Jaw, Saskatchewan.

"I'm Digging a Hole in the Ceiling" in *Something Big Has Been Here* by Jack Prelutsky. Copyright 1990. Reprinted by permission of Greenwillow Books.

"The Little Bear that Couldn't Go to Sleep" by Grace F. Malkin in the 1945 Jan/Feb Issue of *Canadian Nature*. Reprinted by permission of Nature Canada, Ottawa, Ontario.

Rachel Carson. Quote from "The Sense of Wonder" by Rachel L. Carson. Photographs by Charles Pratt. Copyright © 1956 by Rachel L. Carson. Copyright © renewed 1984 by Roger Christie. Reprinted by permission of HarperCollins Publishers, Inc. New York.

Contents

WELCOME TO THE WORLD OF KNEE HIGH NATURE

This is a book for children to use with adults. Parents, teachers and group leaders can share the book with very young children, and older children can enjoy and learn from the book on their own.

We have worked with preschool children and adults for several years at the John Janzen Nature Centre in Edmonton, Alberta. We have been inspired by children who bring with them enthusiasm and a sense of adventure and wonder. How easily they can spot a tiny ant, see a spider crawl under a leaf, hear a duck quack or smell the sap on a sun-warmed spruce tree. How easy it is for us, the adults, to travel from our houses to our cars, to work or to shopping centres without being in touch with our natural environment.

We want to increase awareness and appreciation of nature, to encourage adults to share their knowledge with children, and to help create opportunities for children to share their sense of wonder with adults.

Most of us in North America live in urban settings. We tend to take for granted our dependence on the land from which grow the plants that sustain life. We often forget that everything we use comes from nature: our food, our water, the air we breathe, the paper you are holding, the chair you are sitting upon, the fuel required to heat your home. We should be aware that it is the animals and plants that serve as reliable barometers of the health of our environment. We must never forget our responsibility to the land.

> Come with us now—
> Get to know the outdoors, season by season.
> Come outside,
> Put on your sense of wonder,
> Stretch out your imagination—
> Walk quietly through the forests or prairie,
> Breathe deeply of mountain air,
> Soak in the splendour of a frosty morning.
> Slow down and appreciate our natural world—
> Tread lightly, and understand the life around us.

Understanding and a sense of responsibility grow together in both adults and children. Responsible people will, in turn, make the decisions that will preserve the natural heritage of our planet Earth.

How to Use this Book

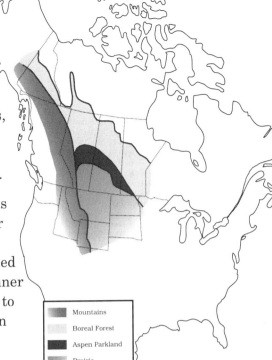

Winter blends scientific information with examples of how we experience nature: facts, stories, poems, games, crafts and pictures. We want adults and children to have fun together outdoors, and we want them to be able to find answers to at least some of their questions.

When you leaf through the book you'll see several kinds of sections. Some explore a **subject**, such as the winter woods or the night sky. Others present the **biology** of groups of animals you might see in winter. We have tried to present these sections in a simple and accurate manner to prepare helping adults to introduce the information to younger children, and to allow older children to read on their own.

Mountains
Boreal Forest
Aspen Parkland
Prairie

All plants and animals throughout the world are classified by their Latin names; this way there is no confusion as to what species is being discussed. We have provided the scientific names for each one we describe. Children enjoy learning the most complex names of dinosaurs, so they may be interested to learn some of these names. For example, the wolf's scientific name is *Canis lupus*. *Canis* is the **genus** name and *lupus* is the **species** name. Several genera (plural for genus) are grouped into a **family**.

Selected **poems, songs and stories** and **follow-up activities** appear throughout as subsections. We hope these get you started, and that you'll develop stories and games on your own. Watch for **neat notes**. We've tried to answer frequently asked questions under this heading.

We've written *Winter* for what we've called the North-West: Alberta, where we live, but also the whole sweep of boreal forest, mountains, parkland and prairie from the British Columbia interior to Saskatchewan and Manitoba, from Alaska and the Yukon to Washington, Idaho, Montana, Wyoming and the Dakotas. But animals, plants, snow and stars don't pay any attention to borders, so you may find the book works well other places, too.

We've made lots of choices. Not every bird or mammal you might see in winter can be found in these pages. If you can't find what you're looking for here, it may be found in one of the other Knee High Nature books: *Spring*, *Summer* or *Fall*. Or check the back of the book for further references.

Most important of all, please use the book. Take it outside. Take it with you on your holidays and on hikes. Use it to compare the tracks you find with the ones illustrated. If it's your own copy, colour the pictures. Or trace them and colour the tracings. And please tell us what you think of *Winter*.

1. Do **dress for the weather**. Comfortable, warm clothes make the difference between a fun time and a miserable time. Wear layers. Make sure boots are not too small; it is better to have them a size too big so trapped air can act as insulation. Mittens are warmer than gloves, because the loose fingers in the mittens can warm each other.

Try chanting "The Mitten Song" as you get dressed:

> Thumbs in the thumb place
> Fingers altogether
> This is the song
> We sing in mitten weather.

Remember that the body loses 40 percent of its heat through the extremities of the head, feet and hands.

2. Do **plan short excursions**, even if it hardly seems worthwhile after the time it takes to get dressed.

3. Do **try to make the weather part of your fun**. If you feel cold do a chickadee huddle. Gather close together with your "wings" fluffed out a little. This is a good time to check for frost nip if the day is cold. If you see whiteness on noses or cheeks, warm the area with a mittened hand or scarf, or head for shelter. A little muscle activity is a quick way to warm up, too. You can flap your arms, jump up and down or hop like a bunny. Do not stay outside when you're suffering from the cold. Short enjoyable experiences build the desire and stamina for longer forays.

5. Do help children understand that, if you see an animal, **it is best to watch it from a distance**. Chasing the animal will stress it and make it waste energy that should be used to keep warm.

6. Do **show respect by following trails**, not littering and not breaking branches unnecessarily. Adults can set a good example for children; children can set a good example for adults.

Are you ready for a winter adventure outside?

- Establish a rally-round call such as: hands up, a chickadee call, a mouse squeak, a woodpecker rat-a-tat-tat or maybe even a coyote howl. When the leader gives the agreed-upon signal, everyone gathers 'round the leader and listens. Have everyone practice responding to the signal at the start of the walk.

- It is always easier to observe things in small groups. Adult helpers are an asset for the adventure.

- Adults don't have to do all the talking. Let the children have time to explore for themselves. Use the rally-round signal if any children wander too far. Use the motto "Less talk, more walk."

- Change activities and pace frequently. After a high-paced activity such as "Coyote Round-Up," try a quiet activity such as "Mouse, mouse come out of your house."

- Go with the flow. If you are really into mice and a jet flies overhead, admire the plane.

Play games outside, or at least one, every time you go out.

- Why not tell stories outside? They do not have to be long or word for word, but the environment enhances the telling. It is also a good way to calm an over-exuberant group. The story can be acted out, if the weather permits.

- Have an ending, such as a short sharing time in a circle to talk about what they liked, a prayer, or just coming together with a positive word about the fresh air or sparkling snow or busy chickadee.

Some Winter Walks

Track Walk

If fresh snow is on the ground, a track walk is a must. Make tracks with your boots. See who can recognize their own boot patterns and then look at others. Make straight lines, circles or follow the leader. Look for tracks of other animals. Ask where some tracks would be found. See if anyone can find bird, mice or cat tracks. Tracks are mostly found near food or the shelter of trees. "Fox and Geese" is a good game for this walk.

Animal Friend Walk

Choose an animal for your outing and pretend to act like the animal. Practice its movements: running, walking, hopping, hiding. See if you can find its favourite food. Can you find a warm place for the animal to rest? "Let's Pretend" and the "Handmade Deer Hat" are good ideas for this walk.

Bird Feeder Walk

Visit a bird feeder to see if it has food. Find out if it is being used. Decorate a tree with goodies for the birds.

Colour Walk

Ask what colours can be seen in winter. Give each child a piece of coloured paper and see if they can find a colour in the woods to match the colour on the paper. Use all colours. You may be surprised at the amount of colour in nature during the winter.

Here
Comes
Winter

Do not disturb

Some Animals Migrate

Animals migrate because winter reduces or eliminates the food available. For example, robins cannot find worms, ducks cannot get at aquatic plants which are under the ice and flycatchers cannot find flies.

Most birds go south. Some travel thousands of kilometers or miles, often following the same route year after year. These routes are called flyways. There are four major flyways in North America for waterfowl. The lesser snow goose travels to California and the Gulf of Mexico from its breeding grounds in the high Arctic. Some pintails migrate to California where many find safety in the Sacramento National Wildlife Refuge, others have even crossed the Pacific to Hawaii. The North-West is the south to some birds, like the snowy owl. They have spent the summer in the Arctic.

Some large mammals like elk, sheep and goats migrate from higher altitudes to lower mountain valleys in winter, where more food is available. Bats migrate, usually to where it is warmer, and then hibernate.

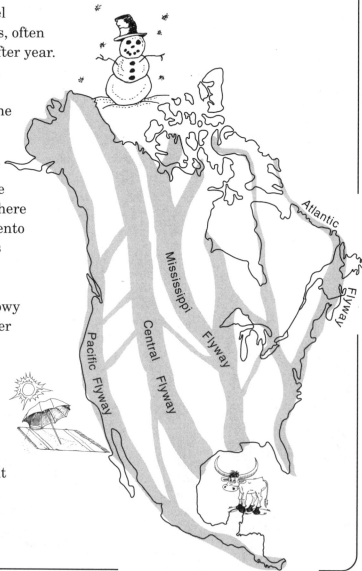

Pacific Flyway

Central Flyway

Mississippi Flyway

Atlantic Flyway

Deep Sleepers (Hibernators)

Winter is a tough time for anything that lives outdoors. Wild animals that cannot migrate south to warmer climates have to endure the cold and the snow. Frost kills the tasty parts of the plants and food is scarce in the winter.

Some animals eat a lot during the fall and put on a thick layer of fat. This layer of fat means they can say good-bye to the cold and lack of food and sleep all winter in the safety of a den. These animals are **deep sleepers** or **hibernators** which means they can lower their body temperature, slow their heart and breathing rates (metabolism) and survive on their stored fat.

Mammals

Bears are happy if there are lots of berries and nuts available in the late summer and fall. This means that they can easily put on a heavy layer of fat that will help them survive the winter. Bears go into their dens in October or November and don't generally wake up, unless disturbed, until March or April. During hibernation, their body temperature drops to about 32°C (90°F), their heartbeat slows from 40 to 10 beats per minute and their oxygen intake is reduced by half. They do not eat, drink, urinate or defecate during their hibernation.

Bear cubs are born in the middle of January or February, while the mother bear is sleeping in her den. Her fat reserves are vital to give her energy for her own survival and for her nursing cubs.

Bats also hibernate. In the fall, they get fat and fly to a sheltered cave to roost. They can sleep for one to two months without waking. Their heart rate goes from 600 beats per minute down to 10 to 80 beats per minute, and their body temperature drops. Hibernation may last seven months for bats, and by the end of winter they have used up all their fat reserves and their little bodies are thin.

Woodchucks and other marmots are also typical hibernators. They put on a layer of fat in the summer, and then each disappears into a burrow in the fall. They do not store food for the winter and rely on their fat reserves for survival. During hibernation their body temperature drops, their heartbeat slows from 100 beats per minute to 15 and they breathe only once every 5 to 6 minutes.

Ground squirrels also hibernate. They feed all spring and summer and then head for their underground burrows. Gradually their body temperature drops, their heart-rates slow down and they appear lifeless. They may wake up for short periods, perhaps to snack on some stored food or to urinate or defecate. They hibernate for about six months and then come out in early spring.

Because their bodies use food so quickly, **chipmunks** cannot put on enough fat to hibernate like the ground squirrels and woodchucks, so chipmunks must gather food and store it in their underground dens. Chipmunks sleep for about six months, but they wake up frequently to snack on their stores of food.

Amphibians and Reptiles

Frogs also hibernate. Wood frogs and boreal chorus frogs bury themselves under leaf litter or in loose soil. This does not give them much protection, and they do freeze. Yet somehow they manage to survive. A low metabolic rate and chemical changes that prevent the formation of ice crystals within their cells help them through the weeks of winter weather. Leopard frogs hibernate at the bottom of rivers or streams, where moving water does not drop below the freezing point.

Garter snakes and rattlesnakes travel to special places to hibernate. These places are called "hibernacula" and may be a deep hole or crack in a hillside. There, the snakes gather in groups, sometimes in the hundreds, to take shelter together.

Earthworms burrow deeper into the soil below the frost line to hibernate.

Plants

Trees can neither fly to warmer climes nor burrow underground. Tree sap goes down into the roots for winter, and the winter buds which have already grown on the tree ready for spring chemically change their free water into unfreezable forms. Evergreen trees like other trees become very resinous and stop growing. When a tree is enduring winter, we say it is dormant.

Seeds have thick coats for protection and a low water content, which help to keep them from being destroyed by freezing.

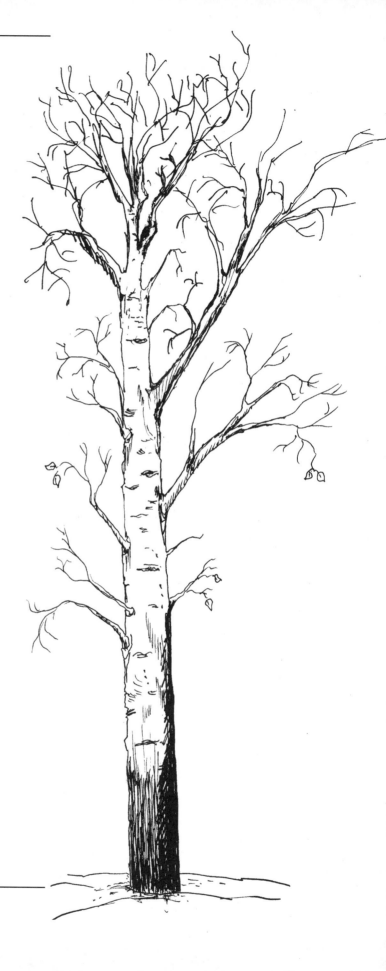

Insects

Where do the insects go when winter arrives?

Queen **bumble bees** are a little fatter than the other bees in the hive. They are often the only ones that survive the cold weather and lack of food. They often hibernate in old ground squirrel holes.

New queen wasps leave the old nests in fall and seek a sheltered spot to hibernate. Winter is a safe time to look more closely at a wasp's nest. Some worker wasps may be found frozen in the old nests.

Ladybird beetles may travel to a sheltered spot and huddle together throughout the winter.

©Knee High Nature

How do insects survive the winter?

Some insects manufacture their own antifreeze (glycerol) which helps prevent their soft tissues from freezing during the long cold winter.

Some insects (in the egg or larval stages) may shelter inside the galls of plants.

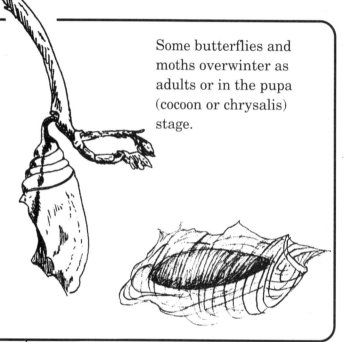

Some butterflies and moths overwinter as adults or in the pupa (cocoon or chrysalis) stage.

Some spiders hibernate in the egg stage; some others as adults.

Can you see the egg sac hidden in the grass?

Light Sleepers

Red squirrels, **gray squirrels** and **flying squirrels** do not hibernate. They remain active all winter. When the weather gets very cold, they seek shelter in underground tunnels or tree cavities and sleep for a few days. They all store food in hiding places called "caches" for winter use.

Red squirrels are frequently seen or heard on winter days scurrying about to their food caches or to convenient bird feeders. As a squirrel bites through the bracts of a spruce or pine cone to get to the seeds, the bracts fall to the ground and accumulate in heaps. These heaps are called "middens." The squirrels may dig tunnels in their middens and live in them during the coldest months.

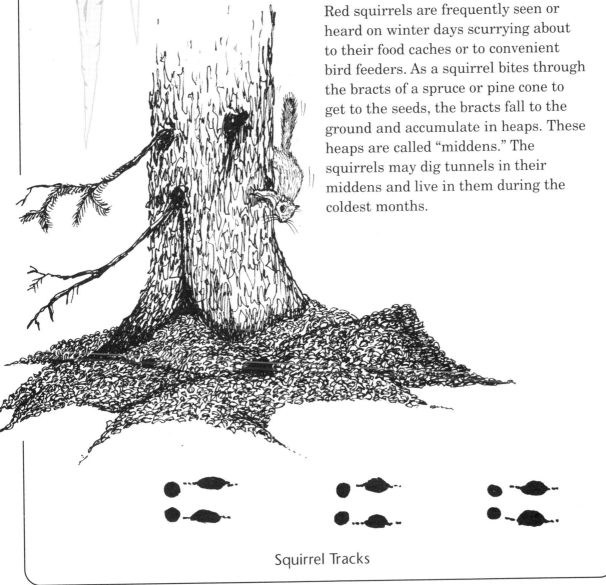

Squirrel Tracks

Porcupines leave trails in the snow that look like troughs, and pigeon-toed tracks leading from their dens to trees. The gnawed areas they leave on deciduous trees are more visible after the trees lose their leaves. Pine-tree bark is one of their favourite foods.

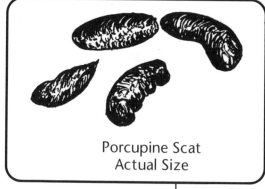

Porcupine Scat
Actual Size

Skunks, **badgers** and **racoons** go into their dens and live off stored-up fat when the weather gets very cold. They do not hibernate; they come out from time to time to search for food. Look for their five-toed tracks in the snow.

Skunk Tracks

Life Under the Ice

Beavers and muskrats live under the ice in ponds and streams.

Beavers survive the winter snug in their lodges with their winter food caches nearby. They stick the branches that make up their winter food piles in the mud at the bottom of their ponds, just a short swim away from the lodge itself. The beaver does not have winter food caches in its more southern habitat.

In the fall, **muskrats** may construct winter houses or burrow in banks. The muskrat does not store large quantities of food for winter, so it must swim under the ice to find food, bite off plants and take them to the nearest "push-up" to eat. Muskrats make several push-ups near their houses or burrows so they don't have to swim far in the cold water. Several muskrats may huddle together in one den to keep warm.

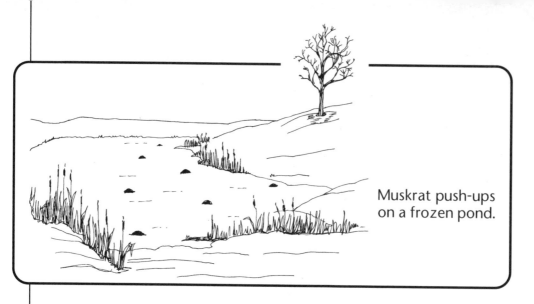

Muskrat push-ups on a frozen pond.

Fish use the available oxygen in the water during the winter. In shallow lakes where snow and ice limit the light necessary for photosynthesis and oxygen production, fish sometimes run out of oxygen and die.

Many pond creatures in adult or immature form are active under the ice all winter, such as water boatmen, backswimmers and scuds.

The Winter Woods

Nibblers
Who's been eating here?

Elk eat the bark of trees when all their favourite food sources are exhausted.

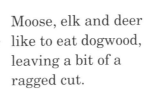

Moose, elk and deer like to eat dogwood, leaving a bit of a ragged cut.

Bunnies nip off twigs, or chew on the bark of small branches. Their sharp teeth nip the branches off cleanly leaving a 45° angle cut.

Lawnmower damage often looks like animal nibbles.

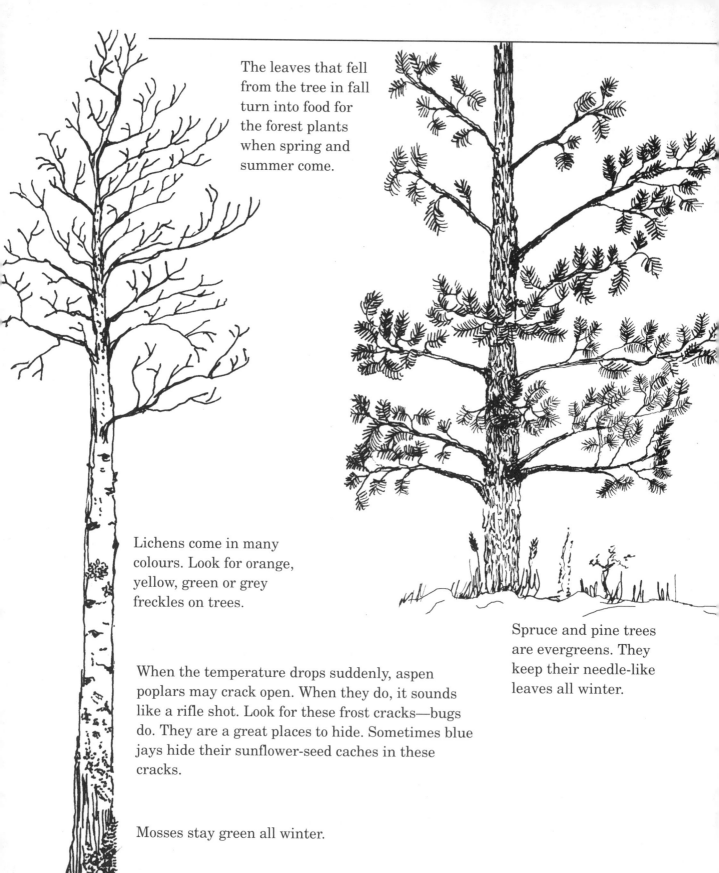

The leaves that fell from the tree in fall turn into food for the forest plants when spring and summer come.

Lichens come in many colours. Look for orange, yellow, green or grey freckles on trees.

When the temperature drops suddenly, aspen poplars may crack open. When they do, it sounds like a rifle shot. Look for these frost cracks—bugs do. They are a great places to hide. Sometimes blue jays hide their sunflower-seed caches in these cracks.

Mosses stay green all winter.

Spruce and pine trees are evergreens. They keep their needle-like leaves all winter.

Spruce needles are single, square and sharp.

Pine needles grow in bundles.

Try learning the difference between pine and spruce by their smell.

Warm the needles between your fingers to release their smell.

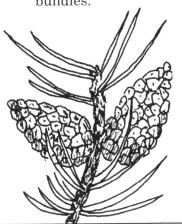

Willows and alders are often about the same size. In winter, female alder trees retain their little catkins which, look like cones.

Winter buds house next years leaves and flowers.

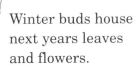

The leaves of some plants, such as wintergreen, stay green all winter under the snow.

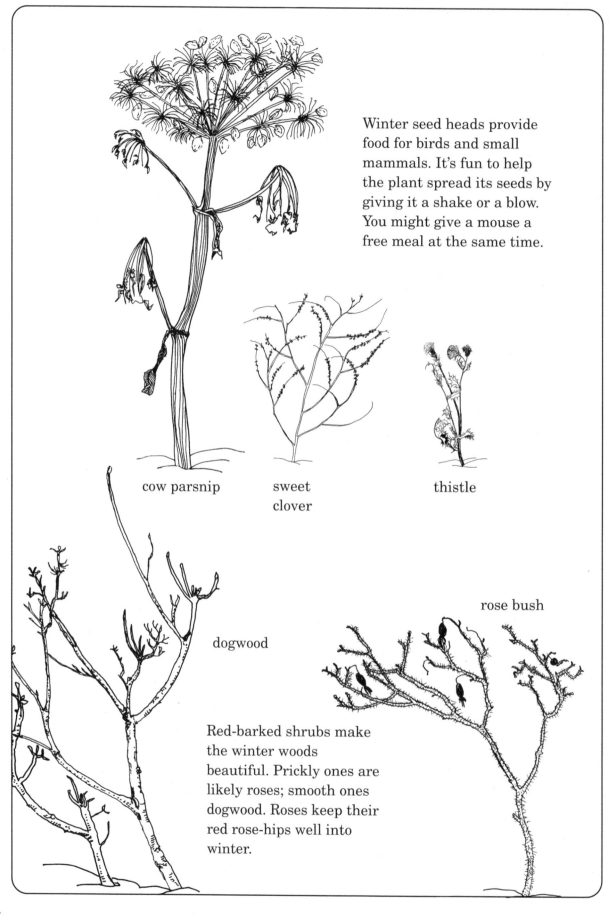

Winter seed heads provide food for birds and small mammals. It's fun to help the plant spread its seeds by giving it a shake or a blow. You might give a mouse a free meal at the same time.

cow parsnip

sweet clover

thistle

rose bush

dogwood

Red-barked shrubs make the winter woods beautiful. Prickly ones are likely roses; smooth ones dogwood. Roses keep their red rose-hips well into winter.

Winter Birds

Winter Birds

Kingdom	Animalia
Phylum	Chordata (animals with backbones)
Class	Aves (the Latin name for birds)
Order	Representatives of these five orders of birds are common in the North-West in winter:

Falconiformes—falcons
Columbiformes—pigeons
Passeriformes—perching birds
Galliformes—grouse
Strigiformes—owls
Piciformes—woodpeckers

Description

Most winter birds are perching birds (Passeriformes) which include the following families: Paridae—the chickadees; Sittidae—the nuthatches; Fringillidae—the grosbeaks, finches, redpolls and crossbills; Emberizidae—the snow buntings and cardinals; Bombycillidae—the waxwings; Corvidae—the magpies, jays and ravens; Passeridae—house sparrows; and Sturnidae—the starlings.

Location

Most birds leave the North-West for the winter. They migrate south. Some birds come from further north to spend the winter here. Birds that stay here all winter must be able to find food and keep warm.

Predators

Owls and hawks prey on other winter birds. Coyotes, foxes and wolves eat grouse and ptarmigan. All members of the cat family, from the domestic "Garfield" to the mountain cougar, prey on birds. The domestic cat is the most common predator at bird feeders.

Can you find the ptarmigan in the picture?

Some birds protect themselves by camouflage. For example, the ptarmigan and the snow bunting are white or mottled white. The ptarmigan turns from brown to white for winter. With only black eyes and a black bill a ptarmigan is almost invisible in the snow.

Food

The birds that stay all winter eat various foods such as seeds, over-wintering insects, berries, small mammals or other birds or dead animals (carrion). At the bird feeder, insect-eaters also eat suet and other forms of animal fat.

Reproduction

Most winter birds breed in spring, but the great horned owl and the gray jay breed in late winter.

Neat Notes

Staying Warm

A bird uses its feathers to make a warm coat. The soft, downy feathers trap air and insulate the bird from the cold, just like a sleeping bag keeps you warm on a cold night.

Some birds, such as the ruffed grouse, jump into a soft, deep snow bank for the night. The snow insulates them from the more severe temperatures above the snow. Ruffed grouse also have feathers on their legs to keep them warm.

Some birds huddle together to share their warmth.

Most birds shiver to keep warm. It takes a lot of food to produce energy to keep warm by shivering.

Most birds find sheltered spots to roost at night and seek protection from the wind.

Some birds conserve internal heat by using a "counter-current heat-exchange system." Warm blood in the artery traveling to the foot is separated by a thin membrane from the vein carrying cooler blood from the foot. The two blood vessels are so close together that the warm blood warms up the cold blood as it passes and very little heat escapes to the outside of the legs. Thus, the feet are kept from freezing but are not so warm as to waste heat energy from the body.

Snow Travel

Ruffed grouse grow comb-like extensions on the sides of their toes that act as snowshoes. They shed them in the spring.

Ptarmigan have feathers covering their legs and toes to keep them warm and to help the birds travel on snow.

Chickadees

Description

What is grey and white and black and calls its name? Answer—The **black-capped chickadee** (*Parus atricapillus*). They are small (13 cm/5") fluffy birds which gather together into small groups for the winter. They flit through the forest calling "dee-dee," perhaps to keep in touch with each other.

In the mountains you may see the **mountain chickadee** (*Parus gambeli*) (12 cm/4 ³/₄"). It has a white stripe in the black cap above its eye.

If you are in spruce woods and hear a chickadee that sounds as if it has a cold, it is likely a **boreal chickadee** (*Parus hudsonicus*) (13 cm/5"). Its cap, back and sides are brown.

Food

Chickadees feed mostly on insects, insect eggs, spiders, seeds and suet.

Neat Notes
In spring, chickadee calls become territorial and sound like, "sweetie-pie, sweetie-pie." In summer, chickadees gradually disperse in pairs and seem inconspicuous in the forest, where they nest in holes in old stumps or dead trees. With the first nip of winter in the air, the regulars return to your backyard feeder.

Nuthatches

Description

The **red-breasted nuthatch** (*Sitta canadensis*) (14 cm/5 ½") looks a bit like a chickadee, but it is slimmer and has a long beak and bluish-grey feathers. It calls a nasal "nyaa, nyaa."

The **white-breasted nuthatch** (*Sitta carolinensis*) (15 cm/6") looks much the same but is a bit larger, has a whitish tummy, calls "quank, quank," and prefers poplar woods.

Food

Like the chickadee, the nuthatch eats insects, suet and seeds. It will take a sunflower seed and stick it in a crack, and then hammer it open with its beak.

Neat Notes
Nuthatches have a characteristic hop reminiscent of a woodpecker. Their most-peculiar and best-known habit is going down a tree head-first. They nest in holes in trees.

Grosbeaks

Description

The only bright-yellow bird to spend the winter in the North-West is the male **evening grosbeak** (*Coccothraustes vespertinus*). It is 20 cm (8") long and has black wings with white wing patches. The female is a dull yellowish grey. Both males and females have large, strong, yellowish beaks (*gros* means "big" in French).

A rosy-red version of the evening grosbeak is the male **pine grosbeak** (*Pinicola enucleator*) (22 cm/8½"). The females and young are orange or grey. Pine grosbeaks have a musical voice. They prefer coniferous woods and will come to a feeder.

Food

Grosbeaks eat buds, berries and seeds. They especially love sunflower seeds and will sit at a feeder deftly cracking open the shells with their strong bills. They munch on the seeds and let the shells fall to the ground. Flocks of colourful grosbeaks make the winter outlay of bags of sunflower seeds seem all worthwhile.

Neat Notes

These birds like to hang around in groups. They figure out where the best feeders are located and then make their daily rounds.

As spring approaches almost all the evening grosbeaks leave for nesting sites in the more secluded and heavily wooded areas.

Redpolls

Description

You will likely notice **common redpolls** (*Carduelis flammea*) sitting in birch trees, eating seeds and letting the left-overs fall to the snow. Redpolls look like streaked chickadees but are a little smaller (12 cm/4¾") and have a daub of red on their heads. Males have a blush down their front, which becomes brighter in early spring.

The **hoary redpoll** (*Carduelis hornemanni*) (12 cm/4¾") is whiter than the common redpoll. Both common and hoary redpolls nest in the Arctic and come south as far as the Canada–US border for the winter, where they are often seen together in flocks.

Food

Redpolls feed on small seeds and bread crumbs. If you live on a farm, save some canola seeds to set out for them—they love such treats.

Finches

Description

The **purple finch** (*Carpodacus purpureus*) is not a winter resident but leaves so late in the fall and arrives so early in the spring that you might notice it in winter. It is a small (15 cm/6") rosy-red bird. The male looks as if he has dipped his head and neck in raspberry jam.

Food

Finches eat seeds in the wild and at the feeder.

Neat Notes The purple finch lives mostly in deciduous woods. Its beautiful song and friendly manner make it a delight to have around.

Crossbills

Description

The **white-winged crossbill** (*Loxia leucoptera*) is a small (15 cm/6") rosy-red bird with white bars on its black wings.

The **red crossbill** (*Loxia curvirostra*) (15 cm/6") is similar but doesn't have the white wing bars.

Food

Crossbills feed on spruce and pine cones. Their bills are actually crossed, uniquely adapted for extracting seeds from between the scales of cones.

Neat Notes

You may first notice crossbills as you are skiing through coniferous woods and see cone scales dropping. Crossbills feed high in the trees, usually in flocks.

©Knee High Nature

Buntings & Cardinals

Description

Snow buntings (*Plectrophenax nivalis*) (18 cm/7") come down from the Arctic in flocks. Look for an undulating mirage of white over a stubble field. Look again: it is the snow buntings' white feathers blending with the snow.

The **cardinal** (*Cardinalis cardinalis*) which looks a bit like a small red blue jay, is found on the eastern edges of the plains where it has strayed in from the eastern forests. Count yourself lucky if it comes to your feeder. Female cardinals are quite brown.

Food

Snow buntings eat seeds.

Neat Notes Snow buntings are often seen flying about in a snow storm when other birds stay put. Sometimes called "snowbirds," the name has become immortalized in one of Anne Murray's songs and in the name of Canada's ace jet flyers.

Waxwings

Description

If a LARGE flock of grey birds comes your way, look for birds (20 cm/8") with black masks, crests on their heads, yellow tips on their tails and reddish-brown under their tails. They are the **Bohemian waxwings** (*Bombycilla garrulus*).

Food

Bohemian waxwings love berries of the mountain ash tree, which has been widely used as an ornamental in cities, towns and yards. As a result, Bohemian waxwings have become very abundant. They also eat wild berries and fruit.

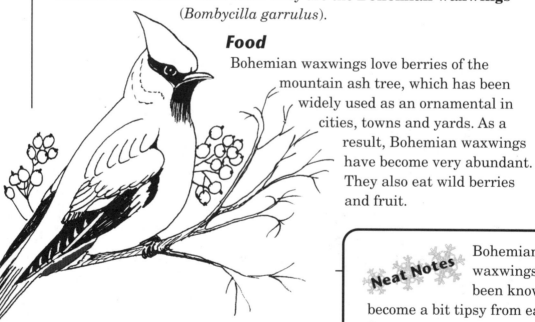

Neat Notes Bohemian waxwings have been known to become a bit tipsy from eating fermenting crab apples.

Woodpeckers

Description

The **pileated woodpecker** (*Dryocopus pileatus*) is a huge (46 cm/18") black woodpecker the size of a crow. It has a big red crest. It flies the way you might imagine the pterodactyl flew, in an undulating path. It makes big holes, often quite low in trees. It also has a big voice. The most famous pileated woodpecker is "Woody Woodpecker."

The **downy woodpecker** (*Picoides pubescens*) is the smallest (16 cm/6$\frac{1}{4}$") woodpecker. It is black and white. The male has a red daub on the back of its head. The **hairy woodpecker** (*Picoides villosus*) looks like a larger version (24 cm/9$\frac{1}{2}$") of the downy but has a bigger beak.

Food

Woodpeckers peck through wood to get to tasty insects in the trees. They do not eat the wood. They uncoil their sticky tongues to feel and catch insects.

Pileated Woodpecker

Neat Notes

Woodpeckers are best known for the "rat-a-tat, rat-a-tat-tat" sound they make.

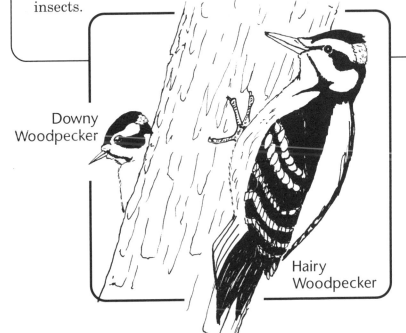

Downy Woodpecker

Hairy Woodpecker

Jays

Description

The **blue jay** (*Cyanocitta cristata*) is large (30 cm/12") and remarkably beautiful, with a crest on its head and a black "V" over its whitish chest feathers. It is found in wooded areas.

In the mountains, you will find the **Steller's jay** (*Cyanocitta stelleri*) (33 cm/13") which is a darker blue. It and the blue jay are the only blue birds around in winter.

Food

Jays eat mostly seeds and insects. At the

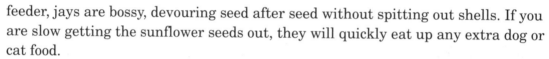

feeder, jays are bossy, devouring seed after seed without spitting out shells. If you are slow getting the sunflower seeds out, they will quickly eat up any extra dog or cat food.

RUPURT

The blue jay has a quieter, gentler cousin, the **gray jay** (*Perisoreus canadensis*) (28 cm/11"). You may be familiar with this fellow at your campsite. Seemingly out of nowhere, this grey-and-white bird comes looking for your crusts, or your unfinished picnic.

Quite similar to the gray jay is **Clark's nutcracker** (*Nucifraga columbiana*) (30 cm/12"), also found in the mountains. It is a bit darker grey than the gray jay, with black-and-white wings and tail, and a bill like a woodpecker's.

Neat Notes

The jay nests in conifer trees. No need for a burglar alarm in the forest with a blue jay around. At the slightest disturbance, off goes the jay calling its piercing, "Thief! Thief! Thief!" to let all know that someone is coming.

Magpies

Description

One common year-round resident is the **black-billed magpie** (*Pica pica*). It is a large (50 cm/20") white and iridescent-black bird with a long tail.

Food

In winter magpies eat just about anything from grains, seeds and garbage, to animals killed on the road. Their clean-up work makes up for their habit of eating other birds' eggs and young.

Neat Notes

Magpies make huge nests in trees or shrubs, and within this large twiggy mass they build mud cups. Inside the cups, the young hatch early in the year. The whole nest is covered with a twiggy roof. Magpies enter through a hole in the side. Magpies make all kinds of raucous squawks and shrill shrieks, but they can also call in soft gurgles.

The magpie has adapted to living with people and livestock and is now common around farms and in cities. It is less common in wilder areas. The magpie's beauty and its elaborate family hierarchy makes this intelligent bird worth observing, but it has been widely persecuted as a nest robber and "garbage bird."

RUPURT

Ravens

In the mountains, in the foothills and in the north lives the **raven** (*Corvus corax*) (63 cm/25"), which looks like a large crow. Like the magpie, it is a first-class garbage gobbler.

©Knee High Nature

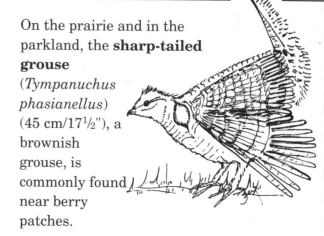

The **Hungarian partridge** or **gray partridge** (*Perdix perdix*) (30 cm/12") is an introduced small greyish-brown partridge with a conspicuous chestnut tail. It is commonly found in small groups in stubble fields, along shrubby country lanes and in urban wild spots where it burrows into the snow in cold weather.

The **ring-necked pheasant** (*Phasianus colchicus*) (76 cm/30") has been introduced. It does best where open grain fields are bordered by dense cover, along creeks or irrigation ditches.

On the prairie and in the parkland, the **sharp-tailed grouse** (*Tympanuchus phasianellus*) (45 cm/17½"), a brownish grouse, is commonly found near berry patches.

The true **prairie chicken** (*Tympanuchus cupido*) was at one time found throughout the Great Plains but is now confined to small areas in north-central United States. It looks like a sharp-tailed grouse but has long feathers on the sides of its neck and a square tail. Some of the traditional dances of native peoples have been inspired from the courtship dances of these birds.

On the southern sage-brush prairie, look for the **sage grouse** (*Centrocercus urophasianus*). This, our largest grouse, is about 63 cm (25") long.

In the deciduous and mixed woods, the **ruffed grouse** (*Bonasa umbellus*) feeds on rose hips, berries, clover and buds. In winter you can see its tracks going from bush to bush. It has feathers on its legs and is about 43 cm (17") long.

In the mountains, look for the **ptarmigan** (*Lagopus lagopus*) (33 cm/13"). It turns white in winter and has feathered feet.

The **blue grouse** (*Dendragapus obscurus*) (50 cm/19½") is found in the foothills and mountains.

In coniferous woods, the **spruce grouse** (*Dendragapus canadensis*) (38 cm/15") is common and feeds on conifer needles. It is a bit darker than the ruffed grouse, and the male has a black chin and bib.

Owls

Description

Owls are commonly seen in winter. The **great horned owl** (*Bubo virginianus*) (55 cm/21 ½") doesn't have horns, but it does have feathers that look like large ears on top of its head.

Some other owls stay all winter. They range in size from the **great gray owl** (*Strix nebulosa*) (75 cm/29 ½") found mostly in coniferous woods to the **pygmy owl** (*Glaucidium gnoma*) (16 cm/6 ½").

Look for the **snowy owl** (*Nyctea scandiaca*) (60 cm/23 ½") sitting on power poles in the open. It comes down from the Arctic to winter here. It is white or white flecked with black.

Food

Owls eat hares, mice and other small mammals and birds.

Great Horned Owl

Snowy Owl

Great Gray Owl

42

Goshawk

Description

A big (60 cm/23½") dark hawk with a white line over the eye is the **goshawk** (*Accipiter gentilis*).

Food

It feeds on hares, grouse, small mammals and other birds.

Neat Notes The goshawk is more common in wild areas than around human habitation. It is a fast-flying bird seen during the day in wooded areas.

Merlin

Description

The **merlin** (*Falco columbarius*) is a little falcon the size of a pigeon (30 cm/12"), sometimes called the pigeon hawk. It is the only common falcon around in winter.

Food

Merlins feed on sparrows, waxwings and other birds.

Neat Notes If something swoops over your feeder very fast—it's likely a merlin. The merlin is common in cities in the winter.

©Knee High Nature

SOME INTRODUCED BIRDS

House Sparrow

Description

The **house sparrow** (*Passer domesticus*) is a very common small bird about 17 cm (6¾") long. The male is rusty brown and grey with a black throat and bib. The female is much more uniformly grey on the tummy with some brown on the back.

Food

House sparrows eat seeds.

Neat Notes

House sparrows are very prolific, producing four to seven young at a time up to three times a year. They take over the nests of many native birds, which has made them very unpopular. They prefer the human environment and are much more common around grain elevators, farm yards and city streets than in the wilderness. Although they are sometimes viewed as pests, one has to appreciate the company of these hardy fellows. They prefer small seeds and like to eat on the ground.

Starlings

Description

The **starling** (*Sturnus vulgaris*) (22 cm/8¾")
in winter is a black bird with light speckles
on its head and back and a dark bill. In
spring, it changes to an iridescent purple,
green, and black with a yellow bill.
Immature starlings are greyish-brown.

Food

Starlings eat seeds.

Neat Notes

The European starling was first
introduced into North America from
Europe in 1890. It is now common. It
commonly over-winters in the southern part of
the North-West and arrives in the north early in
spring. It lays five to seven white or pale-blue eggs
in a nest made of a mass of twigs and feathers. It
competes aggressively with native birds for nesting
sites.

Pigeons

Description

Pigeons or **rock doves** (*Columba livia*) arrived with early
human settlement and have become well established
in the wild. Pigeons look like small chickens.
Generally they are greyish-blue and about
35 cm (14") long.

Food

Pigeons eat seeds. They also like bread
crusts or popcorn.

Neat Notes

Pigeons like to nest on ledges on buildings
but will also use holes in earth banks.

On a cold winter day, look for pigeons sunning on a dark
south-facing roof to get warm. They live in groups and are
found around city streets, under bridges, in farm yards and
especially around feed mills. Their soft voices and
unassertive manners make them a pleasant addition to the
winter scene.

Poems, Songs & Stories

To the Sunny South

Four little birds all huddled together.
The first one said "My, what cold weather."
The second one said, "The sky is getting grey."
The third one said, "Let's fly away."
The fourth little bird never opened his mouth.
So they all flew away to the sunny south.

Author unknown
from the "Preschool Programs Manual"
City of Edmonton, Parks and Recreation

The Chickadees

Harriet Jenks

Five lit-tle chick-a-dees, no room for more;

One flew a-way, and then there were four. Chick-a-dee, chick-a-dee,

hap-py and gay, Chick-a-dee, chick-a-dee, fly a-way.

Four little chickadees, sitting in a tree;
One flew away, and then there were three.
Chickadee, chickadee, happy and gay,
Chickadee, chickadee, fly away.

Three little chickadees don't know what to do;
One flew away, and then there were two.
Chickadee, chickadee, happy and gay,
Chickadee, chickadee, fly away.

Two little chickadees, sitting in the sun;
One flew away, and then there was one.
Chickadee, chickadee, happy and gay,
Chickadee, chickadee, fly away.

One little chickadee can't have any fun;
He flew away, and then there were none.
Chickadee, chickadee, happy and gay,
Chickadee, chickadee, fly away.

by Harriet Jenks
from *The New High Road of Song*

46

The Spruce Tree and the Chickadee

by Florence Holbrook
adapted from "Why the Evergreen Trees
Keep Their Leaves in Winter" from
The Book of Nature Myths

One winter the
chickadee, that little
grey and black and white
bird that calls "chickadee,
dee, dee," decided not to fly
south with the robin and the
goose but to stay in the
North all winter.

©Knee High Nature

Now the chickadee had to find
somewhere warm to go at
night so he went up to the
poplar tree and said,
"Mr. Poplar Tree, may I spend
the winter in your branches?"
"Oh Chickadee" said the
poplar tree, "I lose all my
leaves in winter and you will
be very cold in my bare
branches."

The chickadee flew over to the
mountain ash tree.
"Oh Mr. Ash Tree, may I spend the
winter in your branches?"
"Little Chickadee, I already share
all my berries with big flocks of
waxwing birds. There will be no
room left in my branches for you."

The little chickadee was wondering if he had made the right decision.

Then he saw a beautiful birch tree, you know, the one with the white bark.

"Mr. Birch Tree, may I spend the winter in your branches?"

The birch tree looked at the chickadee and replied scornfully,

"You! In my branches! You might get me all dirty. Get lost Chickadee!"

The poor chickadee was feeling
very dejected when he came
upon a spruce tree.

"Mr. Spruce Tree, may I spend the
winter in your branches?"
"Well, little Chickadee," the spruce tree
replied, "I will try to take care of you.
Maybe, if you get very close to my
trunk, you will be warm enough."

Mother Nature was looking on and after hearing the
response of all the trees she said to the spruce tree,
"You have been so kind to the Chickadee when she needed
your help, I am going to
let you keep your
leaves all
winter
long."

To this day the spruce tree remains green all winter and the chickadee and the
spruce tree have remained the best of friends. Sometimes on a cold winter
morning you can see the chickadee fly out from the branches of the spruce tree.

Best told outside under a spruce tree.

Follow-Up Activities

Beaks and Food

Some birds eat seeds, some birds dig for insects in trees, some birds eat seeds of pine cones and some birds eat meat. Look closely at the beaks of these birds and match them to the food you think they would eat. (Answers on page 54)

1

2

3

4

5

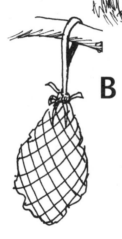

A

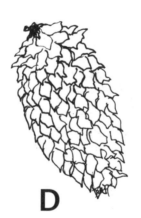

B

C

D

E

How to Tame a Chickadee

To encourage a chickadee to feed from your hand, first establish an active feeding station by filling your feeder regularly. Then one day, when you would regularly fill the feeder, don't. Instead, go to the feeder location and stand very still with the seeds on the palm of your hand. Be patient. If a chickadee hasn't come after five minutes, fill the feeder and try again the next day. It helps to wear the same clothes each time you try. (One man has chickadees who will come to all his guests if the guests wear his jacket.) Within a week you should have some success. Remember to stay still, put the seeds on your hand and put your hand near the feeder. Good luck.

Snow Buntings in a Snow Storm

Snow buntings seem to like snow storms. If you are out in the country, watch for these whitish-brown birds flying near the ground over their favourite weed patch.

Materials:
1 cup Ivory Snow flakes (this is a must)
1/2 cup to 2/3 cup water
Beat with soap flakes until light and creamy — this is the snow.
Heavy butcher wrapping paper
Brown paint

Cut pieces of butcher paper into about 20 x 30 cm (8" x 12") pieces. Place paper, glossy side up, on tables protected with newspaper. Give each child a scoop of snow to spread over the butcher paper. Let the children enjoy using their hands and fingers to spread and smear and cover.

After the children have washed and dried their hands, let them each use a finger dipped in brown paint to daub on five to ten finger print birds against the white background. The brown paint will blend in easily with the snow and produce whitish-brown snow birds. Let the picture dry flat.

A Bird Tree

Birds eat seeds and suet. They also like bread, pastries and peanut butter. Decorate your bird tree (a recycled Christmas tree works well) with some of the following:
- popcorn strings.
- toast cut in shapes.
- onion bags containing suet.
- onion bags cut into stocking shapes, stitched with red double-folded bias tape leaving a loop to hang. Fill with hunks of suet, popcorn balls, bread crusts or cranberries.
- large pine cones filled with a mixture of melted suet, peanut butter and seeds.
- milk cartons with holes cut in their sides for feeding, filled with seeds.
- bleach or plastic pop bottles filled with seeds, with holes cut in the sides of the bottles just large enough for small birds. This is a good way to get food to the small birds if large birds are dominating your feeder.

When you begin feeding birds, make sure to continue for the whole winter, because the birds become dependent on your feeder for food.

Do birds need water in winter?
Not if there is snow, but they do like water if they can find it.

Do birds need grit?
They seem to get enough from roadsides.

Is road salt a problem?
It doesn't seem to be, but don't feed birds salty fat, such as bacon fat.

First Aid for Injured Birds

If you find an injured bird:
- First get a cardboard box with enough room for the bird.
- Pick up the bird gently and put it in the box.
- Close the box and leave it alone for half an hour.
- Take the box outside and open it to check the bird.
- If the bird is dead, phone your local museum or nature centre; they might be able to use it for their displays.
- If the bird seems recovered, release it in a quiet place.
- If the bird is alive but injured, you might want to phone a veterinarian, your local nature centre or zoo, or a fish and wildlife office.

Answers to Beaks and Food

The hawk (1) with its heavy sharp bill eats mice (C).
The woodpecker (2) eats insects found in wood (A).
The grosbeak (3) eats sunflower seeds (E).
The nuthatch (4) eats insects in the wild and suet at the feeder (B).
The crossbill (5) extracts seeds from spruce cones (D).

Snow & Ice

Snow & Ice

Snow is formed by water vapour subliming (going directly from a vapour to a solid) into ice crystals at cold temperatures in the atmosphere. Sometimes this occurs around a dust particle.

Snowflakes are always made up of six-sided, or hexagonal, crystals, because of the shape of water molecules. See if every snowflake really is different.

The more water vapour available, the more detailed and bigger the crystals become. In very cold temperatures, when the air becomes very dry, snowflakes remain small and simple in structure.

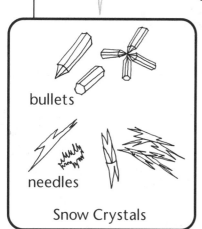

bullets

needles

Snow Crystals

When the crystals get too heavy for the air currents to keep them suspended in the clouds and the temperature between the clouds and the ground stays below freezing, it snows. "Yipee," say the skiers.

Graupel is snow with an ice covering that forms a hard pellet. They sting when they hit you.

Sleet is partly frozen rain or partly melted snowflakes.

Snow next to the ground becomes steadily more compressed because of the pressure of snow above. The snow at ground level is usually crumbly and looks like coarse sugar. It is called *pukak* by some Inuit and *muskowkoonawum* in Cree. Take time this winter and dig down and look at the different types of snow.

Other snow words

Falling snow	*anniu* in Inuktitut	*koona* in Cree
Snow that collects on tree branches	*qali* in Inuktitut	*oskimispon* in Cree
The bowl-like depression in the snow under an evergreen tree	*qamaniq* in Inuktitut	*misposin* in Cree
Snow on the ground	*api* in Inuit	*kooniwun* in Cree

In drier parts of the open prairie, the snow that does fall tends to get blown into depressions, leaving the hill-tops and most fields clear of snow for most of the year. Some animals, such as deer, seek the shelter of the coulees, or small ravines, for cover when resting.

The hare, the lynx and the grouse have adapted to deep snow with snowshoe-like feet.

The moose and deer depend on their long legs.

Snow traps air among its flakes and works like a fuzzy sweater, insulating the ground below from the cooler air above. In very severe weather, when the air temperature is as low as -40° C (which is also -40° F) the temperature at ground level may be as high as -4° C (25° F). The insulating property of snow is vital to the survival of small mammals in winter. Mice, voles, weasels and some insects live just above the soil surface in the "subnivean space."

Sun dogs are also called "mock suns" or "parhelia." In Cree they are called *pecimatim* (literally "sun dog"). Sun dogs are images of the sun on each side of the sun, and at the same elevation as the sun. The inner edges often appear reddish, while the main spots appear whitish. They are most often seen on very cold days when the sun is low on the horizon and there are lots of ice crystals in the air. They are caused by the bending (refraction) of light by ice crystals aligned on their vertical axis. If the ice crystals are more randomly arranged, you see a halo around the sun instead of sun dogs. Be careful not to look directly into the sun—you might damage your eyes.

Ice is frozen water. It is lighter than water, which is why ice cubes float in your glass, and why ice forms at the top of a pond first. Make sure the ice on your pond is thick enough to support your weight before you go skating, and stay away from muskrat push-ups and beaver houses, where it tends to be thinner.

When we skate, the pressure of all our weight on the thin skate blade makes the ice melt. So you don't really skate on ice, you skate on water.

Salt (like pressure) lowers the melting point of ice. That means that if you put salt on ice, the ice will melt, as long as it's not *too* cold. When the temperature gets very cold, salt won't melt ice.

Follow-Up Activities

Snow Diamond Walk

The snow may sparkle on a bright sunny day. Take advantage of a beautiful day and hurry out. Collect some cardboard, elastic and scissors and have the children make snow goggles to protect their eyes when they are outside. Do the craft outside. Dig down in the snow to find the snow diamonds; this is the area mice like. Looking for sun dogs can be fun on this walk.

My Mother Took Me Skating

My mother took me skating
and we glided on the ice,
I wasn't very good at it
and stumbled more than twice.

My mother made a figure eight,
and since it seemed like fun,
I tried a little trick myself
and made a figure one.

by J. Prelutsky
from *It's Snowing! It's Snowing!*

Quinzee Snow Shelter

The **quinzee** is an emergency snow shelter. It is fun to build one in your backyard, and someday knowing how to build such a shelter might save your life.

Scoop snow into a large pile about as high as you are. Wait at least 20 minutes—preferably a few hours—to let the snow settle and harden. Start tunneling at the bottom. Hollow out the inside cave, keeping the walls at least 30 cm (12") thick. It is fun to have a hot-chocolate picnic in this winter home.

Paper Snowflake

Start with a circle of white paper.

Fold it in half. Fold again in thirds, so it looks like a teepee. Cut out a large triangle where the teepee door would be. Nip out designs on the edges. Unfold and hang.

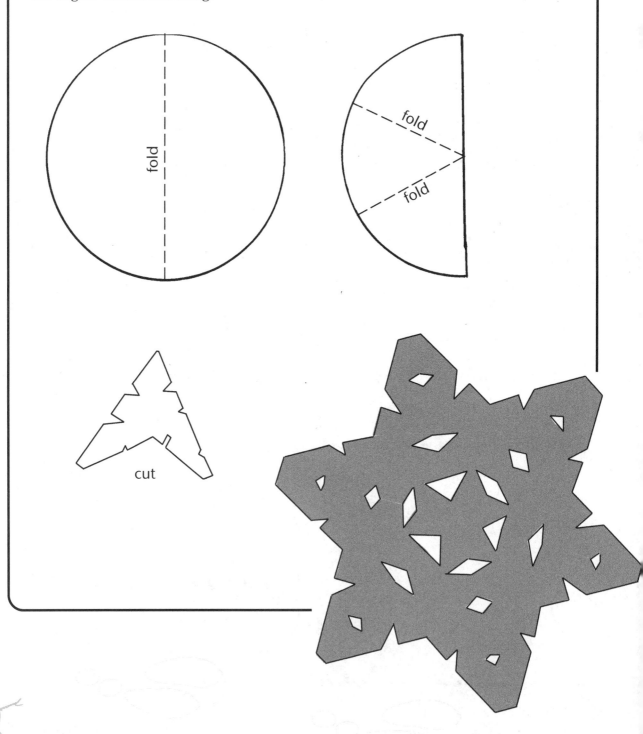

fold

fold

fold

cut

Mice, Voles
& Rats

Mice, Voles & Rats

Kingdom	Animalia
Phylum	Chordata (animals with backbones)
Class	Mammalia (animals that nurse their young)
Order	Rodentia (animals with gnawing teeth)
Family	Muridae (mice, voles and rats)
	Dipodidae (jumping mice)
	Heteromyidae (kangaroo rats)

Description

All mice are rodents. Like beavers, they have large front teeth that keep growing all their lives. To keep these teeth from getting too long, they must continually wear them down by gnawing and chewing. This also sharpens their teeth.

Mice and voles are most easily distinguished from each other by the size of their eyes and ears and the length of their tails. Voles have smaller eyes, ears and tails.

Deer Mouse

House Mouse

Jumping Mouse

3/4 actual size

Vole

Deer Mice

Description:

Deer mice and **white-footed mice** (*Peromyscus* spp.) are the most common and best known mice in the west. They have big ears, big eyes, white feet, white tummies and long, slightly hairy tails.

Location

Deer mice are found in woods, ravines and brushy prairie, but seldom in bogs. They prefer to move into houses, barns or hay stacks for the winter but will build cosy nests in old logs or brush piles.

Food

They eat mostly seeds in the wild and cereals in your pantry. They love cheese.

Predators

Owls, hawks, skunks, weasels, coyotes, foxes, wolves, bears and cats all eat mice.

Reproduction

Deer mice have five or six babies at a time, two or three times a year. The gestation period, the time from mating to birth, is about 24 days.

Deer mice have several nests within their home range.

Baby mice are born naked and blind. They look pink because they have no hair on their skin. They quickly mature under the care of the mother mouse and are ready to live on their own by the time they are three weeks old.

©Knee High Nature

Deer mice store away caches of seeds and grains for winter. They also forage for food. If they venture out onto the snow in search of food, you can recognize their tracks by the distinct tail markings between the foot prints. If they come into your nice warm house, you will first notice some small black droppings near food. Next you might hear some scurrying and gnawing sounds.

However, most mice spend the winter in haystacks or hollow trees and will curl up together in a mound for warmth when the weather gets very cold.

Deer mice are nocturnal; this means they are active at night.

They usually live alone as adults.

Deer mice travel to the same spots again and again, forming trails which are particularly noticeable in snow. Deer mice usually bound, placing the hind feet ahead of the fore feet.

They have a highly developed homing instinct and can find their way home from as far away as three kilometres (two miles).

tracks actual size

hind feet

front feet

tail drag

More Mice

The **northern grasshopper mouse** (*Onychomys leucogaster*), which looks like a deer mouse but eats grasshoppers, is widely distributed in grasslands and desert areas of the North-West.

The **jumping mice** (*Zapus* spp.) have very long tails. They can jump two to three metres (six to ten feet) in one leap. They are found throughout the North-West but they aren't very common. They hibernate in winter so you won't see their tracks in snow.

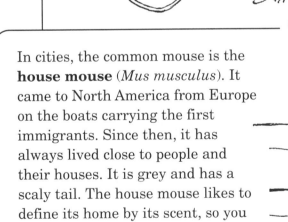

In cities, the common mouse is the **house mouse** (*Mus musculus*). It came to North America from Europe on the boats carrying the first immigrants. Since then, it has always lived close to people and their houses. It is grey and has a scaly tail. The house mouse likes to define its home by its scent, so you can often smell it when it is in your house.

65

Meadow Vole

Description

Meadow voles (*Microtus* spp.) look like mice with smaller ears, shorter tails and smaller eyes.

Location

They live in open areas, preferring the long grass of marshes, ditches and cropland. They don't move into houses but they do like grain bins.

Food

Meadow voles eat tender plant shoots, grains and seeds. They also like to eat the bark of particularly tasty fruit trees in your garden.

Predators

Owls, hawks, coyotes, wolves, foxes, cats, dogs and weasels eat voles.

Reproduction

Four to six young are born several times a year. The gestation period is about 20 to 24 days. Voles mature so fast that some spring babies grow up and breed before summer is over.

Voles are capable of increasing to large numbers quickly and eating as much as their body weight each day, so they can be a nuisance to people when poor weather has delayed harvest and grain is left in the field in swaths. At such times, hawks and owls can feast on voles.

Meadow voles make runways or trails throughout their territory. They maintain these trails by cutting all vegetation at ground level. In the spring, when you rake your lawn, these trails show up as brown mazes.

Voles remain active all winter in the "subnivean space": below the snow and above the ground. They make breathing holes to the surface which can be seen as holes in the snow, frequently with no tracks around them. If they do come to the surface, their tracks can be identified by the lack of a distinct tail marking. Look for meadow vole tracks when you are skiing.

The **red-backed voles** (*Clethrionomys* spp.) are similar to meadow voles in many ways, but their fur is reddish-brown. They prefer life in the forest. They do not make distinct runways, and they roam more freely than meadow voles.

High in the mountains and in the boreal forests, you might find a vole relative, the **northern bog lemming** (*Synaptomys borealis*). It looks like a vole, but biologists classify it separately because its incisors (cutting teeth) are grooved.

Packrats

Description
Packrats or **bushy-tailed woodrats** (*Neotoma cinerea*) are as big as tree squirrels. They look like big deer mice with bushy tails.

Location
Packrats live in cavities of rocks in the mountains or in old barns or cabins.

Food
Packrats eat green leaves, seeds, nuts and roots.

Predators
Owls, weasels, skunks, martens, wolverines, foxes, coyotes and wolves feed on packrats.

Reproduction
Packrats breed once or twice a year and have three to six young per litter.

Neat Notes

Packrats are traders: they sometimes exchange a cone, pebble or stick for shiny objects. If your watch or toy disappears at night and is replaced by a pine cone, you were likely visited by a packrat, not a fairy. Their nests and excrement are very smelly, so if you find your toy, you might not want it back.

More Rats

The **kangaroo rat** (*Dipodomys ordii*) looks like a large jumping mouse with cheek pouches. It lives on the prairie.

The **Norway rat**, also called the **European** or **house rat** (*Rattus norvegicus*), is a large, grey rat. It is found throughout North America. It cannot survive for long in the wild and needs the shelter of buildings. Rigid control measures have kept this unwanted pest from becoming established in some areas.

Mouse Look-Alikes

Do Not Let Them Fool You!

If your cat brings home a mouse and doesn't eat it, look at it closely; it might be a **shrew** (Order Insectivora, Family Soricidae, *Sorex* spp.). Shrews look like small mice with pointed noses. However, they are not even rodents. They eat insects and don't have big front teeth like mice.

Shrews are a common predator and scavenger. They are active night and day, summer and winter in their perpetual search for food. When they come to the surface of the snow, it is often in a clump of grass. Their small tunnels are less than three centimetres (about an inch) across. Tracks show tail markings about half the time, and they are much smaller than mice or vole tracks.

A rodent that lives underground and makes tunnels and hills with no visible entrance is the **pocket gopher** (Family Geomyidae, *Thomomys* spp.), often called "moles." They are about the size of hamsters. Notice their long front claws, well adapted to their underground life.

True moles (**eastern** and **starnosed**) prefer soils where burrowing is easy. They are found only in humid regions, close to the eastern borders of the Great Plains.

Poems, Songs & Stories

Mice

I think mice
Are rather nice.

Their tails are long,
Their faces small,
They haven't any
Chins at all.
Their ears are pink,
Their teeth are
white,
They run about
The house at night.
They nibble things
They shouldn't touch
And no one seems
To like them much.

But I think mice
Are nice.

by Rose Fyleman

Legend of the Pack Rat

Legend has it the only man to actually profit by a Pack Rat's bartering was a prospector who was homeward bound after spending a fruitless summer looking for gold. One night the tired man stretched out beside a commonplace little creek for a sleep; during the night a Pack Rat came, looked over the camp and decided that a piece of rock was a fair trade for a slightly battered tin spoon. In the morning the prospector prepared to make breakfast and looked around for the spoon. That's when he saw the Trade Rat's rock, which was greenish in hue and quite heavy for its size. Breakfast was forgotten as the man feverishly started to explore the vicinity, looking for the spot from which the rat had brought the rock. He did find it: a vein of gold quartz as wide as a city bank! The prospector became a millionaire and lived happily ever after—fairy tales always end that way!

as told by Kerry Wood
from *Birds and Animals in the Rockies*

71

Santa Claus and the Mouse

One Christmas eve, when Santa Claus
  Came to a certain house,
To fill the children's stockings there,
  He found a little mouse.

"A merry Christmas, little friend,"
  Said Santa, good and kind.
"The same to you, sir," said the mouse;
  "I thought you wouldn't mind…

"If I should stay awake to-night
  "And watch you for awhile."
"You're very welcome, little mouse,"
  Said Santa, with a smile.

And then he filled the stockings up
  Before the mouse could wink—
From toe to top, from top to toe,
  There wasn't left a chink.

"Now, they won't hold another thing,"
  Said Santa Claus, with pride.
A twinkle came in mouse's eyes,
  But humbly he replied:

"It's not polite to contradict
  "Your pardon I implore—
"But in the fullest stocking there
  "I could put one thing more."

"Oh, ho!" laughed Santa, "silly mouse.
  "Don't I know how to pack?
"By filling stockings all these years,
  "I should have learned the knack."

And then he took the stocking down
  From where it hung so high,
And said: "Now put in one thing more;
  "I give you leave to try."

The mousie chuckled to himself,
  And then he softly stole
Right to the stocking's crowded toe
  And gnawed a little hole!

"Now, if you please, good Santa Claus,
  "I've put in one thing more;
"For you will own that little hole
  "Was not in there before."

How Santa Claus did laugh and laugh!
  And then he gayly spoke;
"Well! you shall have a Christmas cheese
  "For that nice little joke."

If you don't think this story true,
  Why! I can show to you
The very stocking with the hole
  The little mouse gnawed through.

by Emilie Poulsson
from *Children's Counting-Out Rhymes*

The Mouse

There is such a little tiny mouse
Living safely in my house
Out at night he'll quietly creep
When everyone is fast asleep
But always by the light of day
He'll quietly, quietly creep away.

Author unknown
from *Handbook for Storytellers*

Follow-Up Activities

Snow Blanket

A game for a number of children and at least two adults.

Ask the children, "Do you think it is warm under the snow?
"Let's find out."

Have the adults hold a white sheet high, then ask all the children to be mice and scurry underneath. Bring the sheet down (with the adults inside too) until it's just about touching heads. Talk about how mice live and eat under the snow in winter and how the white blanket of snow protects them from their enemies. Now ask if it is warm under the snow blanket.

Creep Mouse Creep

Chant:
    Creep, mouse, creep!
    The old cat lies asleep;
    The dog's away, the kittens play
    Creep, mouse, creep.

The "old cat" (a child) pretends to sleep on the floor. The "mice" (other children) tiptoe around the cat chanting. At the end of the chant the cat wakes up, and all the mice run behind a line for safety! The child caught by the old cat becomes the next old cat.

from *Preschool Programs Manual*,
Parks and Recreation, City of Edmonton

Parachute Game

For several children and at least two adults.

Have everyone sit or kneel holding the edge of the parachute. Create small ripples by shaking it. This is the snow cover. Have two or three children, without shoes, crawl around under the parachute. They are the mice which are safe and can't be seen by the hunting owls. Now have one child, without shoes, be the owl and crawl around on top of the parachute trying to locate the mice. As soon as a mouse is touched, that child returns to the edge and continues to shake the parachute. When all mice are caught, the owl returns to the edge and the game continues with new children until all have had a turn.

73

Morris Mouse and His Christmas Trees

You will need one 8 1/2" x 11" sheet of green construction paper and scissors. Fold the paper in half on the folding line, and trace the cutting lines from the pattern on page 76. Now you are ready to tell the story as you cut out the tree.

One cold winter night, Morris Mouse crawled up out of his mouse hole. He set out to find a Christmas tree for his family.

Deep in the forest, Morris discovered a beautiful tree. It had a good trunk (cut from 1 to 2), a nice shape (cut from 2 to 3) and it came to a point at the top (cut from 3 to 4). Morris used his sharp teeth and gnawed away at the trunk. Nibble, nibble, nibble. The tree fell to the ground (unfold).

He dragged the tree back to his house. The little mouse tried to get the tree into the long hole that led to his house. "This tree is much too big," said Morris, and off he went to look for a smaller tree (refold the paper).

"There is the perfect tree," he thought. It, too had a good trunk (cut from 5 to 6 to 7), a nice shape (cut from 7 to 8), and came to a point at the

74

top (cut from 8 to 9). Nibble, nibble, nibble, went Morris, and the tree tumbled down (unfold). He pulled it back to his house and tried to get it into his mouse hole.

"This tree is still too big," said Morris, and off he went to look for a smaller tree (refold the paper). There by the pond stood a smaller tree. "Looks good," said Morris. It has a good trunk (cut third tree the same as the other trees), a nice shape, and came to a point at the top. Morris sawed through it with his sharp teeth. Nibble, nibble, nibble. Down fell the tree (unfold paper). The mouse carried it back home and tried to get it into his mouse hole.

"This tree is too big too!" Morris said. Off he went to look for a smaller tree (refold paper).

Near the road, he saw an even smaller tree. It had a good trunk (cut fourth tree the same as other trees), a nice shape, and it came to a point at the top. Nibble, nibble, nibble. Down came the tree, and Morris hurried back to his house (unfold paper). He couldn't get this one into the hole either.

"Even this little tree is too big." said Morris, and he went off again to find a tree (refold the paper). Then he saw a very tiny tree. It had a good trunk (cut fifth tree the same as other trees), a nice shape, and came to a point at the top. Quickly he chewed through the trunk. Nibble, nibble, nibble. Down it fell (unfold paper). Morris picked up the tree and ran all the way home.

"This tree is just the right size," he said. But just as he started down his mouse hole, he saw the four other trees lying in the snow. Morris had an idea!

He took the biggest tree over to Dolly Deer's house and left it by her door (open first tree).

He took the next biggest tree over to Frankie Fox's house and left it by his door (open second tree).

He took the medium-sized tree over to Ruthie Rabbit's house and left it by her door (open third tree).

He took the last tree over to Charlie Chipmunk's house and left it by his door (open fourth tree).

Morris smiled as he carried the tiny tree into his mouse house to surprise Mrs. Mouse and all the little mice (show fifth tree).

by Jean Stangl
from *Paper Stories*

First tree

Second tree

Third tree

Fourth tree

Fifth tree

Folding line

4

9

8

7

3

2

6

5

1

Mouse, Mouse, Come Out of Your House

Find a place where a mouse or vole is likely to live—some long grass in a meadow is good. Form a large circle around this area by joining hands. Drop hands. Make sure there are spaces between children for the mouse to escape. Crouch down and chant together, "Mouse, mouse come out of your house." Watch and listen for a mouse that might come out. If no mouse appears, gently move in closer and repeat.

This activity helps to focus children's attention on where a mouse might live and teaches them to look and listen. Don't be surprised if you don't find a mouse. But then, maybe you will.

by Joy Finlay

Puff Mouse

Materials: grey 3.5 cm (1½") fluffy balls
   grey yarn or elastic (for tail)
   black felt (for nose)
   grey cardboard or felt (for ears)
   craft store eyes (2)
   craft store antennae
(for whiskers) (2 or 3)
   quick-drying glue
(tacky glue)

Glue together. To make the mouse look even more mousey, shave the side and front of the fluffy ball.

Fingerprint Mice

Materials: Poster paint, sponge, paper, fine felt pens or pencils

Mix poster paint, preferably black. Soak a sponge with paint.

Print mice on paper with thumbs, using the sponge as a stamp pad. Draw tail, ears and whiskers on mice with felts or pencils.

Expand this craft to make mouse-covered wrapping paper.

Make-Believe Mice

Materials:

> grey construction paper 8½" x 11"
> pink construction paper for inside ears
> black construction paper for eyes
> two broom straws or long dry grass for whiskers
> 40 cm (16") elastic thread
> scissors
> glue
> tape
> black felt pen

Cut out grey ears from construction paper. Trim the remaining paper into a square. Form into a cone and secure firmly with tape or glue, then trim. Colour on nose with felt pen. Cut and glue pink liners onto grey ears, glue ears onto head. Make tiny holes for whiskers, insert into the cone. Secure elastic below ears and adjust to fit child's head.

PASTE PINK PAPER HERE

PASTE PINK PAPER HERE.

FOLD   CUT   CUT

FOLD   CUT   CUT

Weasels

Weasel Family

Kingdom Animalia
Phylum Chordata
Class Mammalia
Order Carnivora (animals that eat meat)
Family Mustelidae (bad odour)

least weasel

short-tailed weasel

long-tailed weasel

Description

The weasel family includes the weasels, wolverine, otter, badger, fisher, skunk, marten and mink.

All have long bodies and short legs, and they are very agile. They are efficient hunters and can be aggressive and fierce. They all have five toes on their front and back feet.

They all produce a musky smell from their anal glands. The skunk produces the strongest smell of all.

The weasels are the most common active winter resident of this group. Weasels change their colour with the seasons. They turn white in late October and back to brown in spring. There are three weasels in the North-West. The long-tailed weasel, the short-tailed weasel (also called "ermine" or "stoat") and the least weasel. Both the short-tailed weasel and the long-tailed weasel have conspicuous black-tipped tails, even in summer. The least weasel is very small and does not have a black tip on its tail.

Weasels can swim and climb trees.

Because the weasel has such a supple, sinewy body and can move very fast, it can escape many potentially dangerous situations. We use the phrase "to weasel out" to describe leaving a situation when the going gets tough, but weasels can be very tough themselves.

Tracks

When bounding, the forefeet land in the same spot as the hind feet. Sometimes one side is slightly ahead of the other.

Short-tailed Weasel or Ermine

Description
Short-tailed weasels (*Mustela erminea*) are the best-known weasels. They are about as long as this book, including the tail. In winter, their coats are white except for a black tip on the tail. In summer, they turn a chocolate brown on the back but stay white on the tummy.

Location
Short-tailed weasels are found throughout the forested areas of Canada and the northern US and throughout the Arctic.

Food
Like all weasels, the short-tailed weasel is mainly a carnivore. It eats small rodents like mice, voles and lemmings as well as pocket gophers, ground squirrels, chipmunks and birds. It is known around farms for its forays into hen-houses, where it does not stop at sucking eggs but attacks the chickens, sometimes killing far more than it can eat.

Predators
The black-tipped tail of the weasel is an advantage because it distracts hawks and owls from its head where a strike would be fatal. However hawks and owls—as well as foxes, coyotes, larger members of the weasel family and the domestic cat—prey on short-tailed weasels.

Reproduction
Weasels mate about mid-summer but are able to delay development of the embryo (by delayed implantation). The young are born in April or May. There are usually five or six in the litter. The babies are born under dense cover like a windfall or in a den which the mother has taken over from another animal. At first the babies look like baby mice, naked and helpless, but they grow quickly and are ready to hunt on their own in two to three months.

Neat Notes The weasel is trapped for its beautiful white coat, which is called ermine. We now value weasels most for their control of rodent populations.

Other Weasels

The **long-tailed weasel** (*Mustela frenata*) is usually bigger than the short-tailed weasel and does have a longer tail. It is cinnamon brown above and buff below in summer. It is a weasel of the prairie and southern mountains, and it overlaps the range of the short-tailed weasel in the North. Long-tailed weasels feed mainly on ground squirrels. One weasel can have a range as big as one-and-a-half kilometres (a mile) across.

The **least weasel** (*Mustela nivalis*) is the smallest carnivore in the world. It would fit across the width of this page, tail included. It can fit down any hole that allows two of your fingers, so it can go after mice and voles in their under-snow runways. Look out mice! It is found throughout the boreal forest, aspen parkland and prairie.

Other Members of the Weasel Family

Badgers (*Taxidea taxus*) and the **striped** and **spotted skunks** (*Mephitis mephitis* and *Spilogale* spp.) escape the harshness of the cold weather and their predators by sleeping in their dens most of the winter. They are not hibernators, but they sleep for long periods of time.

Mink (*Mustela vison*) and **otter** (*Lutra canadensis*) can move easily and efficiently on land and in water. Both stay brown all winter and usually are found close to water.

Mink look like large dark brown weasels. Their tracks look like a large weasel's and can sometimes be seen near lakes or sloughs where mink spend most of the winter in the gaps left by the ice and water. They feed mainly on muskrats, but when those are not available, mink will travel overland on hare trails in pursuit of other prey.

Otters look like seals with a long tail and an endearing face. Their playful nature even shows up in their tracks, where a few slide marks are often thrown in with

82

their foot pattern. Actually they are so low-slung they drag their bellies in the snow. They prefer to be near fast-moving water that does not freeze, like rapids or below waterfalls. They can chew through ice, particularly thinner ice by a beaver dam, and prey on beaver in their lodges. When you see free water or newly formed ice near a beaver dam, that is a good sign an otter has been around. They occupy huge territories.

Martens (*Martes americana*) look like large brown weasels with bushy tails. Their fur is called "sable." They are seldom seen hunting, but their tracks are sometimes visible from ski-lifts in the Rockies. Look for the circling nature of their tracks, typical of weasels. Their track pattern is a bit like that of cats with the individual track being about 3 cm (1") wide and wider at the toes than the heel. When the marten is bounding, it leaves the typical 2-2 pattern of the weasels. The squirrel, which the marten is probably hunting, leaves a track in the snow which looks like a small rabbit's, with the front and hind prints close together and then a longer space between each set (see page 21).

Fishers (*Martes pennanti*), also called "pecans," are even bigger than martens. They are dark brown in colour and are animals of very wild places in the boreal forest, so they are seldom seen. They are great climbers, and they are very fast. They circle their prey and are one of the few animals which can successfully kill and eat porcupines as part of their diet.

Wolverines (*Gulo gulo*) are big, dark brown to black, muscular and very rare. They look like small bears with long tails. The track, although dog-like, is wider and often shows the fifth toe; it is quite distinctive. They are voracious hunters, and are disliked by some humans because they sometimes raid or spray urine or scent on food caches and trap lines.

Furs

The pelts of the weasel family are some of the most valuable in the fur industry. They have superior insulation value and are often very soft and beautiful. The pelt of the wolverine doesn't frost up, so it is sometimes used as a parka ruff. Human trappers occupy the role of a major predator. In northern communities where the life-style is one of living off the land, well-managed trapping is an important cash crop and furs provide useful clothing, but some people object to trapping.

Poems, Songs & Stories

Pop! Goes the Weasel

All around the cobbler's bench,
The monkey chased the weasel,
The monkey thought 'twas all in fun.
Pop! goes the weasel.
A penny for a spool of thread,
A penny for a needle.
That's the way the money goes.
Pop! goes the weasel.

Traditional

Raven and the Children

Raven found some children who were lost in a blizzard and brought them safely to his igloo. He told them this story to cheer them up until the storm passed.

"There once was a silly old Raven," he began, "who was very hungry. He floated across the sky, searching for food on the ice and snow.

"Raven saw seals and walruses basking in the sunshine," he continued, "but he looked for something daintier and tastier. As Raven flew on, he saw some bushes growing at the side of a stream. He flew closer and then suddenly saw a weasel drinking. Raven's mouth watered at the thought of a tasty little weasel.

©Knee High Nature

"The moment the weasel caught sight of Raven, it dashed across the ground towards its den. But Raven saw the den, flew in front of the weasel, and blocked the entrance.

"The weasel looked at Raven and said, 'Well, I guess you've caught me! I'm very fat and you will have a good meal. Go ahead and eat me! But if you wish to celebrate before you eat, then I will sing while you dance!'

"Raven looked at the weasel and saw that he was indeed fat and beautiful, and realized what a delicious meal he would make.

"Weasel looked at Raven and said, 'Don't be embarrassed. I am proud that I shall be eaten by Raven the great dancer, because I have heard that you are a very fine dancer. Now, if you will dance, I will sing and then you can eat me!'

"Raven was pleased to hear the weasel say such nice things about him.

"'Please,' begged the weasel, 'please dance for me because I have only one wish before you eat me: I wish to see you dance!'

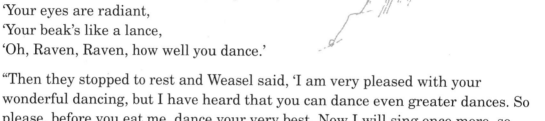

"This pleased Raven so much that he agreed to dance.

"So the weasel sang:

'Oh, Raven, Raven, how well you dance,
'Oh, Raven, Raven, how nicely you prance,
'Your eyes are radiant,
'Your beak's like a lance,
'Oh, Raven, Raven, how well you dance.'

"Then they stopped to rest and Weasel said, 'I am very pleased with your wonderful dancing, but I have heard that you can dance even greater dances. So please, before you eat me, dance your very best. Now I will sing once more, so shut your eyes and dance.'

"Raven closed his eyes and hopped clumsily about while Weasel sang:

'Oh Raven, Raven, look up at the sky,
'As you do your beautiful dance,
'Kick your legs high,
'And make your wings fly,
'As you do your beautiful dance.'

"The moment Raven kicked his legs and spread out his wings, the weasel ran right under him and disappeared into his burrow.

"Raven stopped dancing and stared at the weasel's den. Suddenly Weasel's little nose appeared and Weasel sang this song:

'Oh, Raven, Raven, what a fool you are,
'Oh, Raven, Raven how vain you are,
'You're incredibly dumb,
'Your brain's in your bum,
'Oh, Raven, Raven, what a fool you are.'"

The children laughed as Raven finished his story.

Retold by Ronald Melzack

Follow-Up Activities

Secret Sniffs

Put a strong-smelling object in a small draw-string bag, sock or mitten.

Some examples:

an onion, perfumed soap, ginger, sage, used gym socks, spruce or pine cones, juniper leaves or berries, wet woolen mittens, decaying leaves, mushrooms

Pass the bag with the secret sniff around to each child. Tell the children not to peek and not to guess out loud. When everyone has had a turn, have them guess the smell. Then open the bag and show the object making the smell.

Repeat for two or three sniffs.

Camouflage Walk

Make weasel or snowshoe-hare shapes from white Bristol board. Plastic laminate them to make them waterproof. Hide the shapes near the edge of a trail. Mark the start and end of the trail. Remember how many white shapes have been hidden. Lead the children in small groups to where the trail starts and see if they have sharp eyes like a fox or a hawk and can find the animal shapes.

A variation: While the children hide their eyes, quickly spread coloured squares of paper or toothpicks inside a circle on packed snow. How many can the children find? Then do the same with white or cream coloured squares or toothpicks. Did they find them all as easily?

You might want to try this activity with frozen miniature marshmallows. Celebrate winter by eating a clean, snow-white marshmallow.

Fuzzy Winter Weasel Finger Puppet

You will need a piece of white fake fur, fur or felt the length of the puppet, 2 craft eyes (optional) and a black pen.

Cut out the puppet shape on a double thickness of fabric, making sure the fabric is folded on the fold line. Sew together, fuzzy sides inside, on a machine or with very short stitches. Turn right side out. Make a tail 2/3 the length of the puppet from a scrap of fabric. Sew it together fuzzy sides out. Attach to the top side of the puppet. Glue on craft eyes, or mark eyes with a black marker. Mark on a nose and a black tail tip.

Use cardboard rolls of various sizes, such as toilet paper or wax paper rolls, as a log pile for your weasel to hide in.

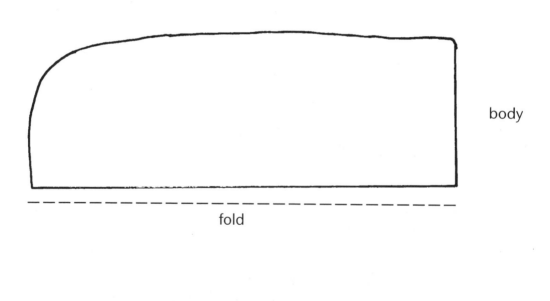

body

fold

tail

fold

Hares & Rabbits

Hares & Rabbits

Kingdom	Animalia
Phylum	Chordata
Class	Mammalia
Order	Lagomorpha
Family	Leporidae
Genus	Lepus (Hares) and Sylvagus (Rabbits)

There are three kinds of hares that live in the North-West: the snowshoe hares, white-tailed jack rabbits and black-tailed jack rabbits. The common name "jack rabbit" is a misnomer as these are hares. Hares in the northern part of their range change the colour of their coats to white in winter.

There are three kinds of rabbits that live in the North-West: the Nuttall's, eastern and desert cottontails. Cottontail rabbits stay much the same brownish-grey colour summer and winter.

Snowshoe Hare

Description

The **snowshoe hare** (*Lepus americanus*) is also known as the varying hare. This hare has very large hind feet, like snowshoes. It changes or varies its coat from brown in the summer to white in the winter. The coat of the snowshoe hare is actually tri-coloured: the outer layer that grows back each winter is white, the middle layer is brown and the inner layer is dark brown. The three layers act as good insulation for the hare. When you walk in the woods, look for this white hare with black-tipped ears.

Location

Snowshoe hares live in mixed-wood forests and aspen parkland in Canada and the northern US.

Food

When winter comes, the hares have to switch their diets from juicy plants to woody trees and shrubs. They eat the twigs and bark of birch, pine, aspen, willow, alder, hazelnut and cherry. They also eat the needles of young spruce and pine trees.

White-Tailed Jack Rabbit

Description

The **white-tailed jack rabbit** (*Lepus townsendii*) is also known as the **white-tailed prairie hare** or **long-eared hare**.

It is about twice the size of the snowshoe hare and is an extremely fast runner. It has very long ears. It is grey-brown in the summer and completely white in the winter. In southern regions where there is little snow, the white-tailed jack rabbit stays grey-brown all year.

The **black-tailed jack rabbit** (*Lepus californicus*) is slightly smaller than the white-tailed jack rabbit and has a large tail with a black stripe on top.

Location

White-tailed jack rabbits live mostly on the prairies and on large grassy clearings in the aspen parkland. Look for them in open areas like school yards, playgrounds, parks and even grassy parts of airfields. They are found in the three prairie provinces of Canada and the north-central US.

The black-tailed jack rabbit also lives in the north-west US, but its range extends into desert habitat. It does not turn white in winter.

Food

They eat mostly grasses, and in winter they also eat twigs and the bark of woody shrubs.

Description

Cottontail rabbits (*Sylvilagus nuttallii, Sylvilagus floridanus,* and *Sylvilagus audubonii*) are smaller than hares and look like baby snowshoe hares. Their ears are shorter and more rounded at the tip than those of the snowshoe hare. They stay brownish-grey all year.

The desert cottontail (*audubonii*) is lighter in colour and has longer ears and legs than the other cottontails.

Location

Cottontail rabbits live in the shrubby areas of creek bottoms, badlands, ravines and coulees. They need grassland habitat with dense bush and low shrubs that provide cover. They have so many predators that good cover is essential. **Nuttall's cottontails** (*nuttallii*) live throughout the prairie region in southeastern Alberta and southern Saskatchewan and western US. The larger **eastern cottontail** (*floridanus*) is widely distributed in the US and overlaps the eastern range of Nuttall's cottontail. The **desert cottontail** (*audubonii*) is found from the Great Plains to Mexico.

Food

Grasses are their favourite food. In winter they eat the twigs and bark of willows and other shrubs.

Predators

Hares and rabbits are the main food for many predators. Coyotes, foxes, lynx, weasels, hawks and owls depend on hares and rabbits for part of their diet. In the south, bobcats and rattlesnakes are also predators.

Neat Notes

Hares and Rabbits

What's the difference between hares and rabbits?

Hare babies are born fully furred, their eyes are open and they are "ready to go" and can hop around just a few hours after birth.

Rabbit babies are born naked, with their eyes closed. They are helpless and stay in a nest until they are about two weeks old.

Hares and rabbits have large front teeth like "Bugs Bunny" that are sharp and can easily cut grasses and twigs and strip bark from branches. In winter, watch in wooded areas for neatly cut "bunny bites" where they have clipped the twigs of many shrubs. They also nibble the bark of young willows, aspens, hazlenut or alder. When the snow is deep, hares can stand on top and reach the tasty twigs and bark of taller shrubs.

Can we see hares and rabbits when we go walking?

If you walk quietly and look carefully you might see some snowshoe hares at the edge of the woods early in the morning or just after sunset.

Watch for their well-worn travel trails through the trees.

When winter storms come, hares take shelter in depressions (called "forms") in the snow. Their white colour helps them to hide from their enemies. Sometimes you can spot them hiding in the shrubbery. Try not to scare them from their hiding place in case there is a predator near by.

Rabbits spend most of the winter finding food and avoiding predators.

Watch for droppings (scat) which will show you the places where they stopped to eat during the night.

Also watch for tracks in the snow. Hares have large feet and their tracks are easy to see in fresh snow.

93

©Knee High Nature

Poems, Songs & Stories

I'm a Little Bunny

(Sing and do actions to tune
"I'm a Little Teapot.")

I'm a little bunny, white and brown.
With one ear up and one ear down.
When I get all frightened I will freeze
In my form as quiet as you please.

Snowshoe Hare

We clomp through the snow
from here to there,
but that isn't so
with a Snowshoe Hare:
his long hind feet
make a very good pair
of snowshoes, fit
for a Hare to wear.

Whisk! He covers
the snow with ease,
dashing along
as fast as you please,
while we go plodding
among the trees,
making foot prints
that reach our knees.

by Aileen Fisher
from *Rabbits, Rabbits*

Hop, Hop, Hop

by Department of Education,
Alberta School Broadcasts
from *Your Listen and Sing Song Book* 1958-59

Hop hop hop Mis-ter Kan-ga-roo; Hop hop hop Mis-ter Rab-bit too.

Hop hop hop Mis-ter Tree Toad small, Hop hop ev'-ry bo-dy o-ver the wall.

Little Brother Rabbit

One autumn Wesakchak felt very sad. All through the summer there had
been no rain. The prairie grass was burnt brown and dry. The little streams
had grown smaller and narrower, until at last not a drop of water was left.
The animals, finding no grass to eat and no water to drink, had all gone to
the far north-west, where the Great River came down from the mountains.
For they knew that along its banks they would find grass to eat. Wesakchak
wondered if the Great Spirit was angry with the people of the plains when He
sent them these long, hot days and nights. Why did He let the animals go
away from them, leaving the hunters no game to kill? The little children were
crying for food, and the warriors had grown thin and sad during this summer.
And now the fever had come, and in the lodges many sick were lying.

Wesakchak felt that he must do something for his people, so he asked the Great Spirit to show him where the animals lived, so that he might tell his hunters and save the lives of all in the tribe. Then Wesakchak took his canoe and carried it until he came to the Great River. Getting in, he paddled for many days and many nights. He watched all the time, to see if any game came near the banks, but he saw no sign of any.

At last, after he had gone many hundreds of miles, he felt so tired that he knew he must rest. He drew his canoe up to the side of the river and made a lodge from the branches of trees. Here he slept during the night, and when morning came, he arose quite rested. Before he had gone to sleep that night he had noticed that the clouds hung low, and he had wondered if there would be snow in the morning. Now, when he came forth from his lodge, he saw that all the land was white. During the night a heavy fall of soft snow had come, and all the trees and the prairie were covered with it.

Wesakchak was greatly pleased, for this was just what he had hoped for. Now he would be able to see the marks of the animals and trace them to their homes. Going down to the river, he was delighted to find the trail of a deer, who had been down for a drink. There were also the marks of the other animals, and now Wesakchak made up his mind to follow these trails and find where the animals were living. He set out, and tramped for many miles. The sun arose and shone on the snow, making everything a dazzling white. But Wesakchak did not mind, and tramped on. At length he knew he was near the place where the animals were

living. He took a good look at the trees, so that he could tell the hunters where to find them. Then he turned to hurry back, for he wished to let them know as soon as possible. He tramped on again for a long time, but he did not seem to be getting any nearer to the river. He stopped and looked around. Everything was glistening white, and nowhere could he see a river or a tree. He wondered if he were lost and what he would do, for he knew that if the sick people did not get food soon, they would die. He turned in another direction and travelled for some time. Then stopping, he looked around once more. Again all was glistening white, dazzling his eyes so much that he could see nothing. He knew now that he was snowblind, and felt very sad indeed, for how could he get the news to the hunters in time to save the sick ones, when he could not find the river and his canoe? If only there was something to guide him, —some dark object that he could see; but everything was a dazzling whiteness.

Just then he noticed a little, brown object in front of him. As he looked at it, it hopped a few steps ahead and then stopped.

"Oh, Brother Rabbit," called Wesakchak, "I am so glad to see you. I cannot find the river and I want to get back and tell the hunters where the game is living."

"Let me guide you," said the rabbit. "Keep watching me, and you can see my dark fur against the white snow."

As he said this he hopped away, and Wesakchak, looking only at the little, dark body, was able to follow, till at last they reached the bank of the river. The canoe was there, and Wesakchak stepped in at once, glad that he would now be able to carry the good news to the warriors and hunters. Before he paddled away he turned to the rabbit and said:

"My little Brother Rabbit, you have been very kind to me, indeed, and through your kindness the lives of our tribe will be saved. In return for this your brown fur shall become white as the first snowfall, so that no one will be able to see your body against the snow. In this way you may protect yourself, and people will know how kind the rabbit was to Wesakchak."

As he spoke, the rabbit's fur suddenly became pure white, and it looked like a little ball of snow near the bushes. Wesakchak smiled when he saw this and said:

"Your enemies will need to have sharp eyes now, little Brother Rabbit, for you will give them many a long chase over the winter prairies."

from *Thirty Indian Legends*

Follow-Up Activities

Hug Tag

This game stresses the relationship of bunnies and trees. Designate a few children to be "trees" and ask them to spread themselves about the game area. The other children can be the "bunnies," and the helping adult can be the "hawk." Bunnies hop about until the hawk calls, "Here comes the hawk." Bunnies then run to the "trees," and are safe if they find a tree to hug or crouch beside. More than one bunny can share a tree. Reverse the roles of trees and bunnies and play again.

Caution: Very young children can be upset if they are caught, so it is best to have the helping adult be a really slow hawk.

Move Like a Bunny

Bunnies have all kinds of movements.

To the beat of a drum or just clapping hands you can play follow-the-leader doing the special movements of bunnies:

—Hop, Hop, Hop: Front, Back, Sideways
—Crouch
—Freeze
—Explode (with a leap from hiding place)
—Zig and Zag

97

Paper Roll Bunnies

Cut ears out of paper and glue or staple them onto a white toilet-paper roll. Glue a cotton ball onto the back for the fluffy tail. Make a face with crayons or markers.

Reversible Masks for the Seasons

Use half of a paper plate for a mask and the other half to make ears. Colour one side brown for summer, leave the other side white for winter. Staple on ears. Cut a notch for the nose. Locate eyes to fit, and cut out fairly large holes for eyes. Staple elastic to the sides of the mask.

Alternate Mask: Use a lightweight paper plate. Cut one straight cut into the centre. Overlap pieces slightly and staple at bottom. This gives a three dimensional effect for the nose. Continue to add eyes, ears and elastic to wear as a mask.

98

Deer Family & Friends

Deer Family & Friends

Kingdom	Animalia
Phylum	Chordata
Class	Mammalia
Order	Artiodactyla (even-toed)
Suborder	Ruminata (cud chewers)
Family	Cervidae (deer family)
	Bovidae (sheep and goats)
	Antilocapridae (pronghorn)

Description:

The deer family belong to the order Artiodactyla. *Artios* means "even-numbered" in Greek; *daktyla* means "toes." The deer family, worldwide, has more than 30 members. Five members are native to the North-West: **white-tailed deer**, **mule deer**, **caribou**, **elk** (or **wapiti**) and **moose**. Members of the deer family are typically brown, slender and long-legged. All have large ears, large eyes and short tails. The white-tailed and mule deer are both about a metre (three feet) tall at the shoulder. Note the size comparisons among females in the rest of the deer family (males are bigger):

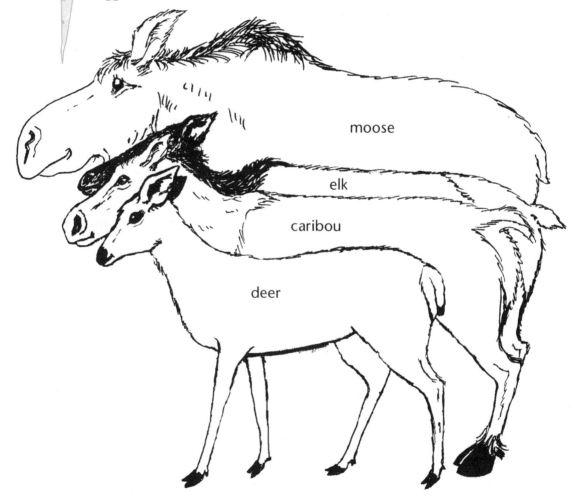

moose

elk

caribou

deer

Food

All members of the deer family are plant eaters (herbivores).

They do not have upper front teeth but instead have a hard dental pad against which the lower front teeth can bite.

The front teeth and dental pad are used for tearing the vegetation. The back teeth are used for grinding and chewing.

Neat Notes

All members of the deer family are ruminants, and all have *four* stomachs. They eat food quickly, chewing just enough to swallow. The food then passes to the first and second stomachs, where bacteria break down the cellulose of the plants. This breakdown produces a lot of gas which is relieved by belching.

The animals return the remaining food, called "cud," to the mouth for more chewing, then swallow it again. The food then moves on to the third and fourth stomachs, where digestion is completed.

Members of the deer family eat early in the morning and again in the evening. They hide and rest during the day, and chew their cud, as the mule deer in the illustration is doing.

Antlers

All males of the deer family have antlers made of solid bone, which grow in the spring and summer and are shed in the winter. Females do not have antlers, except the female caribou.

Young males, born in the spring, develop soft "buttons" on their heads, and by the time they are six months old the buttons may have reached about three centimetres (one inch) in length.

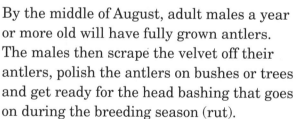

In the early spring, the new growth of the antlers is covered with a fuzzy skin called "velvet." In this early growth period, the antlers are spongy and very tender, and they can be easily damaged.

By the middle of August, adult males a year or more old will have fully grown antlers. The males then scrape the velvet off their antlers, polish the antlers on bushes or trees and get ready for the head bashing that goes on during the breeding season (rut).

After the rut, sometime during the winter, the antlers fall off.

Each succeeding summer, males grow heavier and longer antlers until they reach their largest size when the animal is five or six years old. As the animal grows older, he produces smaller antlers. The number of points or "tines" does not indicate age; teeth are the best age-indicators, since they grow in a regular sequence, and the roots show growth rings, like trees.

Babies (Fawns and Calves)

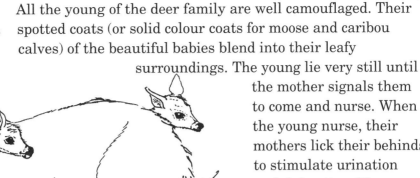

All the young of the deer family are well camouflaged. Their spotted coats (or solid colour coats for moose and caribou calves) of the beautiful babies blend into their leafy surroundings. The young lie very still until the mother signals them to come and nurse. When the young nurse, their mothers lick their behinds to stimulate urination and defecation. The mother then eats the urine and feces to help hide the scent of her baby from predators.

Rut

"Rut" is the name given to the breeding or mating season of the deer family, which takes place in the fall. It is the time of year when the males fight each other for dominance, and to attract females.

During the rut, males use their antlers to see who is biggest and strongest. Males rarely have a serious fight unless there is a confrontation between two who are evenly matched. Sometimes just pushing and shoving are all that is necessary to decide who is stronger. Occasionally a headlong rush and crash of antlers can result in locked antlers with dire results: one or both deer can die from exhaustion or be eaten by predators if they cannot free themselves.

The Rut	ELK	MOOSE	CARIBOU	DEER (mule and white-tailed)
	September	October	October	November

Green-Up Time

After a long winter looking for food, munching twigs and avoiding predators, deer—particularly the pregnant females—long for the new, green spring grass and leaves which are rich in protein. If spring is late in arriving, deer can miscarry their fawns as a result of malnutrition. Those that do give birth may not have enough milk to support their newborn fawns.

When the deer are in open areas feeding on new shoots they are easy to spot. If you are lucky, around sunset or sunrise you might see moose, elk or deer feeding in open areas near cover.

Be a detective

Since members of the deer family are so shy and so clever at hiding in the woods, you must look for evidence that they have been out and about. Playing detective and looking for tracks in the mud and snow is lots of fun. And, when you are walking in the woods, you may come upon the droppings (scats) of an animal. Guessing which animal passed this way is always a challenge. The drawings of tracks and scats below will help you.

Tracks and Scats
half size

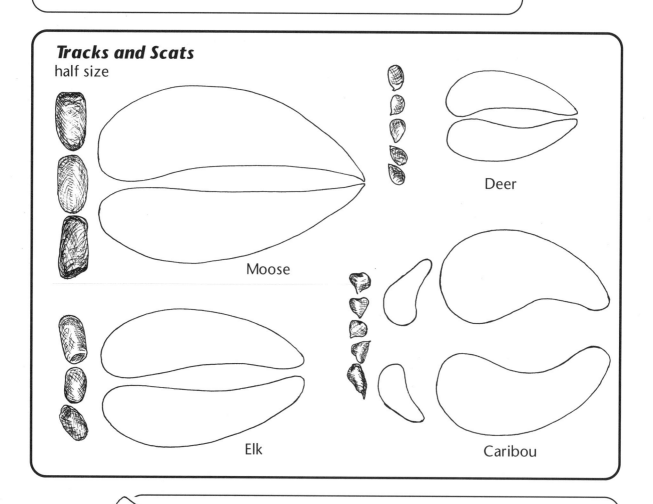

Moose

Deer

Elk

Caribou

Deer Crossing Signs

Watch for these road signs as you travel. They are located near areas where trees offer cover on both sides of the highway. These are habitual pathways for the deer. Be alert, because these signs are posted where there have been several collisions between vehicles and members of the deer family.

104

White-tailed Deer

Description

The **white-tailed deer** (*Odocoileus virginianus*) has a long, wide, bushy, brown tail that hides its white rump. When danger threatens, it raises its "flag," or tail, and the white rump and white underside of the tail become very visible.

The eye ring, band around the muzzle, belly, chest and spots on the hind legs (which are scent glands) are all white. When you see a deer, look for these white markings. If these areas are not white, you may be looking at a mule deer.

The coats of white-tailed deer are reddish-brown in summer and greyish-brown in winter. Deer have keen noses and sharp eyes. White-tailed deer's eyes are located more to the front of their heads than those of mule deer, so white-tailed deer can see ahead as they run through the woods. The very small white metatarsal scent glands (2.5 cm/1") on the outside of its hind legs above the hooves are distinctive features of the white-tailed deer.

The antlers of the white-tailed deer consist of two main beams with up to five or six single tines that grow upward from each beam. The large brow tines are very noticeable.

Male deer are called bucks, and females are called does. The young are called fawns.

brow tine

metatarsal gland

Location

White-tailed deer are very adaptable to a variety of habitats and are wide-spread in southern Canada and most of the US.

Food

White-tailed deer eat twigs, especially those of aspen poplar, snowberry and rose. They also eat leaves, horsetails, peavines, buds, grass, grain, mushrooms, fruit and bark. In winter they eat twigs, as well as alfalfa and other crops. They are commonly seen in and around alfalfa fields or hay stacks in winter.

Predators

Coyotes, dogs, wolves and cougars prey on white-tailed deer.

Reproduction

Twin fawns are born in late May or early June. The gestation period is about seven months. Low temperatures and prolonged snow cover can be disastrous for the young and old.

The Rut

The peak of the breeding season is generally mid-November.

Movement

 White-tailed deer have graceful leaps and bounds that take them to clumps of trees to hide. They can cover eight metres (26 feet) in one leap, jump over obstacles about two metres (6½ ft) high and run up to 45 km/hour (28 mph). They are very clever at hide and sneak. They can disappear quickly in the trees and can even crouch and crawl to avoid hunters. Both white-tailed and mule deer can "freeze" and thus remain invisible. Many live quietly and go unnoticed in cities, in places where there is good cover.

Mule Deer

Description:

Mule deer (*Odocoileus hemionus*) have large mule-like ears fringed with black. They have wider faces than white-tailed deer. Their eyes are set more to the sides of their heads (like bunnies'), allowing them to see all around the open spaces and hills where they prefer to live.

Mule deer have a stockier appearance than white-tailed deer.

They have dark foreheads and dark eyebrows, especially males. They have short, white, rope-like tails with black tips resting on their white rumps.

They also have large (12.5 cm/5") brown metatarsal glands on the outside of each hind leg.

Their antlers have two main beams with tines that fork and then fork again. The antlers have very small brow tines.

This "muley" buck has four points or tines on each side.

Location

Mule deer are found in western Canada and the western US. They range from the Yukon to Mexico. They like open spaces, rolling, hilly terrain associated with shrubs and mixed woods, and badlands.

Food

Mule deer eat many of the same foods as white-tailed deer. They also like juniper needles and sage.

Predators

Cougars, coyotes, wolves and dogs prey on mule deer.

Reproduction

Mule deer does most often have twins, but mule deer are less productive than white-tailed deer. Many white-tailed fawns may breed before their first birthday. Mule deer fawns generally breed in their second year. "Muley" fawns are usually born in June.

The Rut

Mule deer breed in November just like white-tailed deer.

Neat Notes

Movement

Mule deer bound in a stiff-legged way with all four feet off the ground (called "stotting"), with their tails down. They look like an animal riding on a pogo stick. They can bound easily and quickly over rough or steep terrain.

Mule deer are bolder and more curious than white-tailed deer. This can lead to trouble, particularly during hunting season.

Deer can have a tough time during the winter. If the snow is deep they use a lot of energy making trails to their twiggy food. Fortunately, during the summer they build up their fat reserves. Fat acts as insulation for winter and is a way of storing food. The deer start to grow long, thick hair in summer, so that by winter they have warm coats.

Caribou

Description

There are two types of **caribou** (*Rangifer tarandus*) in North America: **woodland** and **barren ground**. Caribou are medium-sized members of the deer family with long legs, large hooves and hair on their noses. Both males and females grow antlers.

The woodland type is larger and sturdier than the mule deer, and bulkier than the barren ground caribou. Its winter coat is brown, thick and long with a whitish mane. Its outer coat consists of long guard hairs. The undercoat has fine, short hairs—very warm for cold weather. The summer coat is generally dark brown in colour.

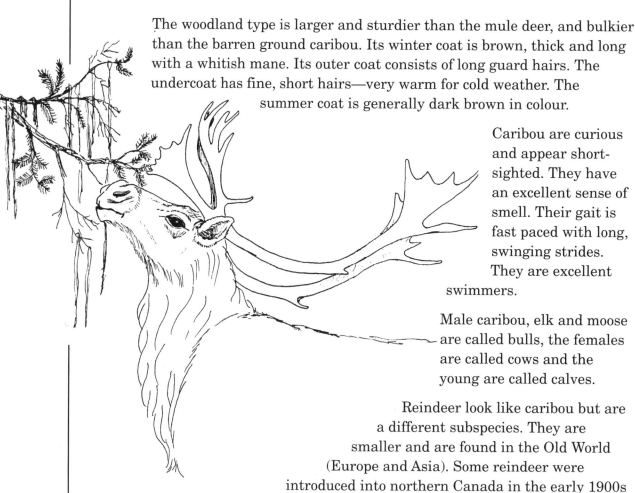

Caribou are curious and appear short-sighted. They have an excellent sense of smell. Their gait is fast paced with long, swinging strides. They are excellent swimmers.

Male caribou, elk and moose are called bulls, the females are called cows and the young are called calves.

Reindeer look like caribou but are a different subspecies. They are smaller and are found in the Old World (Europe and Asia). Some reindeer were introduced into northern Canada in the early 1900s to be used as domestic animals.

Location

Historically, caribou were found throughout Canada and the north-eastern US, but as settlement advanced woodland caribou numbers declined. Most woodland caribou now live in the boreal forests of Canada (except in the Maritimes).

There is a mountain variety of the woodland caribou that lives in the mountains of Alberta and British Columbia and ranges into Idaho.

The barren ground caribou live in the tundra of northern Canada and Alaska. They are often on the move to find food, or to escape from predators and insects. Some herds stay on the tundra all year, while others migrate into the boreal forest for the winter.

Food

In summer, caribou eat green grass, leaves and lichens. In winter they prefer lichens but will eat shrubs and grasses. They need old forests that provide them with ground lichens and the black lichens that hang from spruce trees (old man's beard).

Predators

Wolves particularly, and also bears, prey on caribou.

Reproduction

Caribou usually have one calf, and only rarely twins. The gestation period is seven to seven-and-a-half months. Calves are born in late May to early June.

The Rut

The breeding season is in October.

Neat Notes

Caribou calves remain with their mothers for about a year. The cow-calf groups are sociable. In the winter, all ages gather for mutual protection. Adult bulls often separate from the cow-calf group and in so doing do not compete for food with the now-pregnant cows. Pregnant female caribou grow antlers that help them compete for better feeding areas during winter. They drop their antlers around calving time.

The feet of caribou are unique. The hooves spread out in summer making it easier to walk in spongy muskegs. In winter, the soft pads of the hoof deteriorate and the pad area becomes concave (curved inward), exposing the sharp edge of the hoof. This gives the caribou a better grip on the snow and ice.

Can you tell which animal is on the back of the Canadian quarter?

Description

The **elk** or **wapiti** (*Cervus elaphus*) is a large deer. In all seasons its pale yellow rump is very distinct. The tail is short and almost unnoticeable. The elk's head, neck, legs and shaggy mane are usually dark-coloured.

In summer, both sexes have deep reddish-brown coats. In winter, their coats are lighter in colour, which may explain why the Shawnee Indians called them "wapiti," which means "white deer."

The antlers of the male elk or wapiti are elegant, large and spreading. They consist of two long, round beams which sweep up and back, each usually bearing six tines.

Location

At one time, elk were the most widely distributed member of the deer family on the North American continent. They occurred from coast to coast and from Mexico to northern Alberta.

They are now found mainly in the foothills and mountains of the western US and south-western Canada.

Food

The elk is a grazer and primarily a grass eater. When necessary, it will feed on woody plants such as snowberries, willows, saskatoons and aspens, and it will also feed on broad-leaved plants such as peavines.

Predators

Wolves, coyotes, bears and cougar prey on elk, particularly on the young.

The Rut

In early September, the bulls start the rut by searching for female elk. Younger bulls are driven from the cow-calf herds as older bulls try to gather a harem of 15 to 20 cows. The older bulls spend most of their time fighting off other bulls that are trying to steal cows from their harems.

Fall is a hectic time for bull elk. If they are not fighting, they are busy holding their cow harems together.

By the fall equinox (September 21), the breeding process reaches a peak as the bulls bugle, fight off other bulls and hold onto their harems.

By the second week in October, the breeding season is over and the bulls go their separate, solitary ways or gather in small bachelor groups to recover from the rut.

Reproduction

Elk calves are born in early June. Usually only one is born; twins are rare. The gestation period is eight to eight-and-a-half months. The calves have spotted coats and hide under shrubs for the first two to three weeks of their lives, only coming out to nurse. They often squeal when frightened.

When the calf is strong enough to travel, the mother elk and calf join other cows and calves on the summer range. The calves nurse until fall and stay with their mothers until spring.

Neat Notes

The elk bugle sounds like a deep whistle and terminates in a grunt or a series of grunts. The bugle advertises the bull's whereabouts, attracts cows, and serves to guard the cows. If a hunter is successful in "calling in" a bull elk, he had better be prepared for a hostile and aggressive animal.

The mother elk are always alert to danger. When alarmed they give a loud, sharp bark.

The elk moves elegantly, holding its head and neck high as it walks or trots.

The best time to see elk in parks is during winter, when elk cows, calves and bulls congregate on their winter ranges. They prefer clearings where food is available and where there is safety in numbers.

The bulls drop their antlers in late winter.

Native wild animals can most often survive the extremes of the seasons without requiring special winter feeding and water, as do cattle.

Moose

Description

The **moose** (*Alces alces*) is the largest member of the deer family. Moose have the largest antlers.

The moose is dark brown and has very long legs. It has a large and long nose; its upper lip is thick and hangs over its lower lip. It has a shoulder hump and a "beard" (properly called a "bell") hanging from its throat.

This animal has to be seen to be believed. The males have wide, heavy antlers shaped a bit like hands with the fingers spread out.

Location

The moose is an Old World animal that came across the Bering land bridge from Asia to the New World about 150,000 years ago. It is now found in the mountains, foothills and forests across Canada. They also live in the Rocky Mountains as far south as Utah. On good range, the population density of moose is one moose per quarter section or two moose per square kilometre. The moose is the least gregarious member of the deer family, which means it doesn't spend much time with other moose.

Food

Moose love twigs, especially willow and dogwood. Moose will also eat broad-leaved plants, leaves, and the bark of shrubs and trees. In marshy areas, moose eat willow and also feed on duckweed, waterlilies and other water plants.

Predators

Wolves, bears and cougars prey on moose.

The Rut

In September or early October males start looking for females. The male moose call sounds like a grunt. The female moose also calls at this time. Her call is a softer "moo" and grunt. Mating takes place around the first week of October. Then the animals go their separate ways.

Reproduction

Single calves or twins are born in May or June. The gestation period is eight months.

Motherhood is a top priority for female moose. They are very attentive to—and can be very protective of—their newborn calves. The mother and calf should be avoided until the calf is a few weeks old and can run more easily with its mother. Many a person has been treed by a protective mother moose.

The baby moose stays with its mother for the first year.

The long legs of the moose enable it to run easily through deep snow. The moose likes forested areas, especially after a burn, when new vigorous growth is coming up from the forest floor and burnt spars or deadfall are common. If necessary, the moose can high step and run its way quite gracefully through the deadfall, eluding pursuing wolves.

OTHER HOOFED MAMMALS

Pronghorn

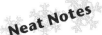

Description

Pronghorn (*Antilocapra americana*) have chunky brown-and-white bodies and long, slim legs. They have large white rumps and white stripes under their necks. The males (bucks) have distinctive black jaw patches and grow two upright horns, each with a prong projecting forward. The females (does) grow smaller horns or may not grow horns at all. Their eyes are large and have thick lashes to shade them from the sun.

Location

Pronghorn live on the prairies. Their range is now limited to southern Alberta, southern Saskatchewan, Montana, the Dakotas, Wyoming and south to Mexico.

Food

Pronghorn feed on many different plants and shrubs, but sagebrush and sage are their most-favoured foods.

Predators

Coyotes, bobcats and long winters with deep snow are pronghorns' greatest enemies. Golden eagles sometimes prey on their fawns, which are born in May.

Neat Notes

Before Europeans settled the west, there were about 35 million pronghorn (commonly called antelope). By the 1920s they were on the edge of extinction. Fortunately, good wildlife management has now increased their numbers to about one million.

The pronghorn is the fastest of all North American mammals. Its hooves are cushioned to absorb the shock of its long stride over hard ground. Even a five-day-old pronghorn fawn can run faster than a person.

They have remarkable vision. They often feed in small groups, meaning more eyes are available to spot their predators.

Pronghorn is the only horned mammal that sheds the sheath that covers its horn every year.

The song "Don't Fence Me In" applies to the pronghorn. Historically, they roamed the unfenced grasslands freely. They are great runners but are not great jumpers. They can wiggle under fences or go through openings, but they have not adapted to jumping over man-made obstacles, or to some of the other changes human settlement brings.

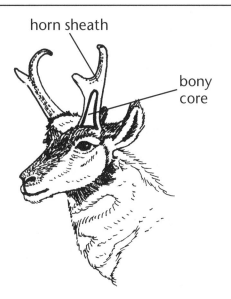

horn sheath

bony core

Rocky Mountain Bighorn Sheep

Description

Rocky Mountain bighorn sheep (*Ovis canadensis*) are brown stocky mammals, each with a large white rump patch. Both males (rams) and females (ewes) grow horns. The rams' horns grow bigger each year and curl in a circular form. The ewes grow smaller, upright horns that look like those of mountain goats. Horns of both ewes and rams continue to grow throughout their lives and are never shed.

Location

Bighorn sheep are wilderness animals that live on grassy slopes close to rocky cliffs. They need the rocky cliffs to escape from their predators such as wolves, coyotes, mountain lions and bears.

Food

Bighorns eat grasses, sedges, legumes and some shrubs.

Neat Notes The rams use their horns for spectacular head-on clashes to compete for dominance. Their skulls are well fortified for protection from the impact of other rams.

They have exceptional eyesight and climbing ability.

Rocky Mountain Goats

Description

Rocky Mountain goats (*Oreamnos americanus*) are white, stocky mammals with white beards. Both males (billies) and females (nannies) grow thin black horns. The horns of both are similar and do not grow longer than about 30 cm (12"). They do not shed their horns.

Neat Notes Goats use their horns to compete for dominance by raking the sides of their opponents. The sharp points of their horns can cause serious injury.

Goats have large oval hooves with cushion-like pads surrounded by a hard shell which help them to be great climbers. Their large dew claws provide a good grip when going down steep cliffs.

Location

Mountain goats are wilderness animals that live in remote rugged, mountainous, regions. They need rocky cliffs to escape from the same predators that prey on bighorn sheep.

Food

Goats eat grasses, sedges, willows and conifers.

119

©Knee High Nature

WINTER IS A TOUGH TIME

All hoofed mammals grow thicker coats in fall that keep them well insulated from the winter's cold. Most go into the winter with some stored fat that they have put on during the late summer and fall, but some of the males lose weight during the fall rut. If the winter is long and the snow is deep, both males and females will have eaten most of the available food on their winter ranges and used up most of their stored fat by spring. If more nutritious food is slow to appear in spring, they may die from malnutrition or be easy prey for predators.

The wintering ranges of hoofed mammals are absolutely necessary for their survival. Roads or other major developments on these critical winter ranges can make it impossible for them to survive.

Mountain goats generally continue to live high in the mountains during the winter—they must be near rocky cliffs to escape from predators.

Goats tend to be solitary in winter, although mother goats will have their kids with them until the following spring.

They take shelter from winter storms in caves or rocky overhangs. If the snow is deep they will move to lower elevations.

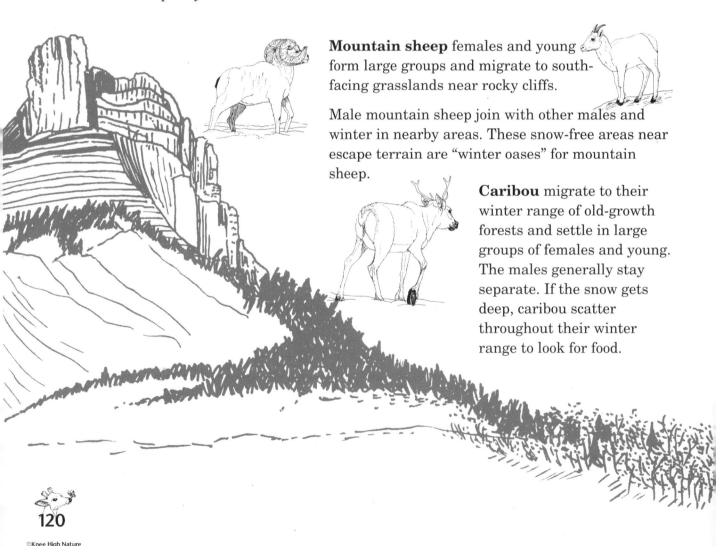

Mountain sheep females and young form large groups and migrate to south-facing grasslands near rocky cliffs.

Male mountain sheep join with other males and winter in nearby areas. These snow-free areas near escape terrain are "winter oases" for mountain sheep.

Caribou migrate to their winter range of old-growth forests and settle in large groups of females and young. The males generally stay separate. If the snow gets deep, caribou scatter throughout their winter range to look for food.

Elk. When the winter snows begin, cows, calves and most bulls migrate down to their winter ranges where they can be seen in large herds. Some of the older bulls stay at higher elevations.

Moose are usually solitary, although when snow is deep they may concentrate in one area. Mother moose keep their calves with them until spring. New growth areas, following fire or logging, provide a nutritious supply of food. Moose also need forested areas to give them shelter from severe weather conditions.

Mule deer and **white-tailed deer** move to winter ranges where food is most plentiful. Tree cover for shelter during bad weather is very important. In severe weather, they remain bedded, resting and ruminating, for longer periods to save energy. They need good browse (leaves, stems and buds) for winter feeding. When they have to eat the older and tougher parts of a shrub they may have digestive problems.

Bison (sometimes called "buffalo") have long coarse guard hairs and a thick woolly undercoat to keep them warm in winter. They often face the wind because they have more hair on their head, shoulders and front legs than on their rear. Bison use their huge heads to sweep the snow away to expose their food, which is mostly grasses and sedges. They are well adapted to survive severe winters and can even digest poor quality forage.

Once there were millions of bison ranging the Great Plains and northern forests, but now they are confined to large parks, sanctuaries and game farms.

Pronghorn live on the prairies in all seasons. In winter they move, or migrate, 3 to 150 kilometres (about 2 to 100 miles) to winter ranges where there is less snow or where sagebrush, a favourite food, is available.

Poems, Songs & Stories

How the Fawn Got Its Spots

Long ago, when the world was new, Wakan Tanka, The Great Mystery, was walking around. As he walked, he spoke to himself of the many things he had done to help the four-legged ones and the birds survive.

"It is good," Wakan Tanka said, "I have given Mountain Lion sharp claws and Grizzly Bear great strength. It is much easier now for them to survive. I have given Wolf sharp teeth and I have given his little brother, Coyote, quick wits. It is much easier now for them to survive. I have given Beaver a flat tail and webbed feet to swim beneath the water and teeth which can cut down the trees and I have given slow-moving Porcupine quills to protect itself. Now it is easier for them to survive. I have given the birds their feathers and the ability to fly so that they may escape their enemies. I have given speed to the deer and the rabbit so that it will be hard for their enemies to catch them. Truly it is now much easier for them to survive."

However, as Wakan Tanka spoke, a mother deer came up to him. Behind her was her small fawn, wobbling on weak new legs.

"Great One," she said. "It is true that you have given many gifts to the four-leggeds and the winged ones to help them survive. It is true that you gave me great speed and now my enemies find it hard to catch me. My speed is a great protection, indeed. But what of my little one here? She does not yet have speed. It is easy for our enemies, with their sharp teeth and their claws, to catch her. If my children do not survive, how can my people live?"

"Wica yaka pelo!" said Wakan Tanka. "You have spoken truly; you are right. Have your little one come here and I will help her."

Then Wakan Tanka made paint from the earth and the plants. He painted spots upon the fawn's body so that, when she lay still, her colour blended in with the earth and she could not be seen. Then Wakan Tanka breathed upon her, taking away her scent.

"Now," said Wakan Tanka said, "your little ones will always be safe if they only remain still when they are away from your side. None of your enemies will see your little ones or be able to catch their scent."

So it has been from that day on. When a young deer is too small and weak to run swiftly, it is covered with spots that blend in with the earth. It has no scent and it remains very still and close to the earth when its mother is not by its side. And when it has grown enough to have the speed Wakan Tanka gave its people, then it loses those spots it once needed to survive.

by Michael J. Caduto
and Joseph Bruchac
a Dakota Sioux story
from *Keepers of the Animals: Native American Stories and Wildlife Activities for Children*

Rudolph the Red-Nosed Reindeer

Rudolph, the red-nosed reindeer
Had a very shiny nose,
And if you ever saw it
You would even say it glows.
All of the other reindeer
Used to laugh and call him names.
They never let poor Rudolph
Join in any reindeer games.
Then one foggy Christmas Eve
Santa came to say,
"Rudolph, with your nose so bright
Won't you guide my sleigh tonight?"
Then, how the reindeer loved him
And they shouted out with glee,
"Rudolph, the red-nosed reindeer,
You'll go down in history."

by Johnny Marks, 1949

Follow-Up Activities

Run and Hide

Deer have long legs and can run fast and hide in the bushes and be safe from danger.

Find the nearest woodlot. Set boundaries. A helping adult can be "it". Help the children hide behind trees or bushes. When "it" calls "Here I come," "it" will walk down the path *once* to see whom he or she can find. If "it" sees anyone he or she will call out their names and the children will come and join hands with "it." "It" will walk past once again with his helpers to see if they can find anyone else.

If there are any children left who have not been found by "it," call them to stand up where they hid. Everyone can discuss how they hid so well.

Let's Pretend

Discuss what deer look like: big ears, big eyes, black shiny nose, pink tongue. Let's pretend we are deer and go for a walk.

When the leader calls:

STOP—listen for danger with your big ears.

EAT—taste twigs (pretend to eat the deer's twiggy food).

DOG BARKING—run to the nearest tree and hide behind it.

PEOPLE TALKING—all the deer must "freeze," as still as an ice cube.

Rudolph Needs a Nose
A version of "Pin the Tail on the Donkey"

Have each child make a big red round nose from paper. Put a big drawing or picture of Rudolph on the wall.

Have the children stand behind a line not too far from the wall. Blindfold the first child (a felt mask is more comfortable than a scarf). As the first child walks toward the wall with his or her paper nose held in front of him/her, have a helping adult ready to tape the nose to the wall at the first place the child touches with his outstretched hands.

Try to appreciate how Santa found his way in the dark and how Rudolph's shiny nose made the trip so much easier.

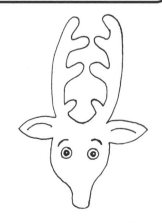

Oh Deer!

This is an excellent habitat game from "Project Wild" which can be simplified for younger children. The children become "deer" and components of habitat.

All deer need good habitat to survive: food, water and shelter. Ask the students to count off in fours. Have all the ones go to one area; all the twos, threes and fours go together to another area. The ones become deer. Have the "deer" line up facing away from the habitat group.

When the "deer" are looking for food, they should clamp their hands over their tummies. If looking for water, they should put one hand over their mouths. And if the deer are looking for shelter, they should hold their hands over their heads like a roof. The deer may choose to look for any of the three habitat components but must not change what they are looking for until the beginning of the next round.

The twos, threes and fours become the habitat. Each child chooses which habitat component they will be during that round: food (hold your hand over your tummy), water (put one hand over your mouth) or shelter (hold your hands over your head like a roof). Have the habitat children and the deer children stand in two lines with their backs to each other, about 6 metres (20 feet) apart.

The leader counts "1, 2, 3," and on 3, each group turns to face the other, holding their hands in their chosen positions. Habitat cannot move, so the deer group will *walk* towards the habitat with their hands in position looking for a match. The deer that find a match take the habitat person back to the deer line. Those who do not find a match "die" and remain as habitat.

Try again until everyone gets the idea. Encourage comments about any imbalances that happen. You might want to record the number of deer at the beginning of the activity and record how many deer survive at the end of each round.

from "Project Wild Elementary Activity Guide." Ottawa, Canadian Wildlife Federation. 1985.

Handmade Deer Hat

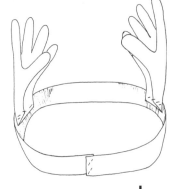

Trace patterns of children's hands on brown Bristol board. Fold double and cut out to obtain two matching hands. Cut out headband, staple on the "antlers," and tape or staple to fit.

In real life, antlers curve, so you can fold the thumb over to the pointer finger and staple in place at the base of the antler.

Antler activity: Have the children wear their deer hats. See if the "deer" can move carefully through trees or bushes without touching the branches. If there are no trees nearby, set up an easy obstacle course with chairs to go over and a table or two to go under.

Deer Treat Bag

Take a brown paper lunch bag.
Cut out antlers.
Add a face with crayons, markers or coloured paper.
Staple antlers at an angle if you wish.

Candy Cane Deer

Use pipe cleaners for antlers. Glue on two felt eyes and add a black or red pom-pom nose.

Spruce Cone Deer

Antlers can be cedar twigs or any other branching twig.

Legs can be popsicle sticks broken in half. Use a strong glue when gluing the head (half spruce cone) to the body (whole spruce cone). An elastic band can hold the cones in place until the glue dries. Glue on paper or felt eyes.

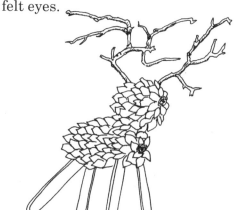

Rudolph Puppet Play

Have each child make a deer puppet on a stick. Use twigs or paper for the antlers and tape them on. One child can be Rudolph, the rest can be ordinary deer. The teacher can have a Santa puppet. Sing "Rudolph, the Red-Nosed Reindeer" and act out the story.

Wolves
Coyotes & Foxes

Wolves, Coyotes & Foxes

Kingdom	Animalia
Phylum	Chordata
Class	Mammalia
Order	Carnivora (animals that eat meat)
Family	Canidae (dogs)

Description

Wolves, coyotes and foxes all have hairy ears, bushy tails, a simple digestive system and large canine teeth, just as dogs do. They have four toes and a pad on each foot which gives them a secure grip on rough terrain. Like dogs, they walk on their toes. Their toenails do not retract and are visible in their tracks, unlike a cat's claws, which retract. There is a fifth toe on each front foot, but it does not reach the ground. Dogs, wolves and coyotes are closely enough related to interbreed.

Wolves, coyotes and foxes breed once a year, unlike dogs which breed twice a year. Wolves, coyotes and foxes have dorsal glands at the base of their tails, while dogs do not.

canine teeth of red fox

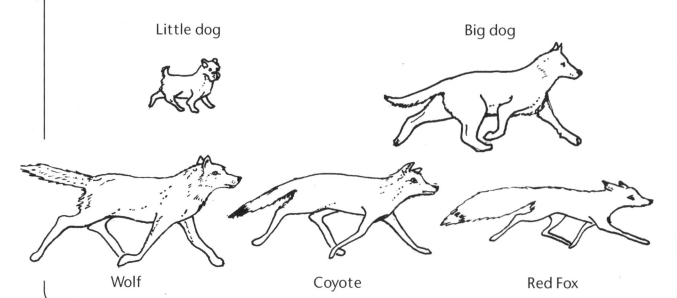

Little dog

Big dog

Wolf

Coyote

Red Fox

	SIZE & WEIGHT	FOOD	SOUNDS	SOCIABILITY	MATING
Wolf	large (45 kg) (100 lbs)	deer, moose, elk, caribou, beaver	howl	pack	pair for life
Coyote	medium (13 kg) (28 lbs)	hares, mice, carrion & young ungulates	yip & howl	pair	pair for several breeding seasons
Red Fox	small (5 kg) (11 lbs)	hares, mice carrion	bark	solitary	pair for 1 breeding season

A wolf resembles a large husky, but with a narrow chest, a long body and a narrow head. The wolf carries its tail straight out. A husky has a broad chest and usually carries its tail curled over its back.

The hind legs of the wolf, coyote and fox swing in the same line as the front legs when they are running or trotting, while a dog places its hind legs between its front legs.

Wolves, coyotes and foxes are most easily distinguished from dogs by their elusive behaviour—they try to stay away from people.

Reproduction
Wolves, coyotes and foxes keep the same mate for at least one breeding season. In fact, coyotes often keep the same mate for several breeding seasons, and wolves often keep the same mate for the life of the partner. All have a structured family life and an elaborate communication system.

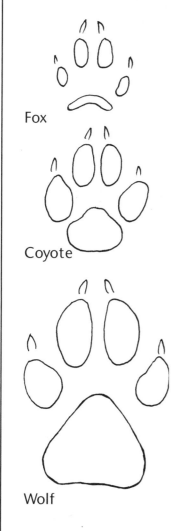

Fox

Coyote

Wolf

Tracks

Large dog tracks can be as big as those of a wolf, while small dog tracks can be smaller than foxes'. Most dog tracks are about the size of a coyote's.

The dog's track is more round and spread out than the oval compact track of the coyote. The dog's front toenails are more spread out than those of the coyote's, which are close together and point forward.

Dogs' tracks show front and back feet while coyotes' back feet land on top of the front prints and form a fairly straight line, like cats' tracks.

Coyotes are on the look-out for food, and their tracks tend to reflect this, while dogs usually just sniff for fun.

Dog

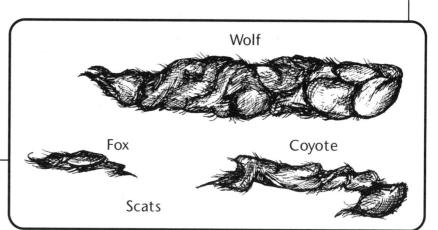

Wolf

Fox

Coyote

Scats

Cat tracks don't show any toenails because cats usually retract their nails when walking. The space between the centre large pad and the toe pads is more pronounced and rounded in a cat track than in a dog track.

The northern **lynx** (long eartufts and black-tipped tail) and the southern **bobcat** (short eartufts and a black-barred and black-tipped tail) make large cat-like prints. The lynx's will often show hair marks around the paw prints. The cougar or mountain lion makes a huge cat-like print about the size of a wolf's!

Wolves

Description

Wolves (*Canis lupus*) look like large dogs with penetrating eyes, expressive faces, long legs, big feet and narrow chests. Their thick fur is usually tawny grey but can be black or white. Their facial fur is long, in a mask from the bottom of the ears to around and under the muzzle. Males average 48 kg (106 lbs.) and females 41 kg (90 lbs.). Wolves are about 160 cm from tip to tail, which makes them about the height and weight of a five-foot-tall human.

Location

Wolves are found throughout the forested, sparsely populated regions of the North and the mountains, generally in densities of no more than one per 26 square kilometres (10 square miles). Wolves are not found in settled regions because they are severely controlled by humans along forest borders near agricultural land.

Food

Wolves are the most important northern predators of large mammals including moose, deer, elk, caribou and bison, and, less often, bighorn sheep, mountain goats and beaver. When close to agricultural land they occasionally prey on cattle, sheep and horses. They also eat small mammals but these do not contribute significantly to their diet. It takes a lot of food to satisfy a wolf.

Predators

People, grizzly bears and cougars compete with wolves for the same food and people and grizzly bears will kill wolves. Wolves will also kill each other when desperate for food. Wolves are not considered a food source by any predator.

Reproduction

Wolves are able to breed by the time they are 22 months old. Mating occurs in February. The gestation period is 60 to 65 days and the pups are born about the end of April. A long courtship precedes mating; wolves often pair for life. There are about six pups to a litter.

Pups

Neat Notes

Baby wolves are called pups, and they look like dog puppies. Their first home is a deep den dug into the side of a hill, usually near water. The den has been made by their mother with help from the pack. Wolf pups are born blind. They usually open their eyes and begin to explore after ten days. By three weeks they appear at the den opening and can be seen playing like dog pups. They chase their tails, tumble about with each other and play tug-of-war with pieces of bark. A social order quickly develops among the litter, with the biggest usually the most dominant.

While the mother wolf cares for the pups, the other adult wolves in the pack stay within sight of the den where they can watch for intruders. The father, along with the other wolves in the pack, assumes responsibility for feeding the mother and pups. After four weeks the pups are ready for wolf-chow. This is the food the wolves bring back from a hunt—they carry it in their stomachs, not their mouths. All a pup has to do is rub its muzzle against that of the adult wolf and the wolf regurgitates warm, partly digested wolf-chow. The pups solicit food not only from their parents but also from other members of the pack. When the pups are four weeks old the mother wolf, called the bitch, may get a break from the demands of motherhood. Occasionally an adult member of the pack will stay behind and pup-sit while she joins the hunt.

At 10 weeks the adults take the pups from the den to rendezvous sites. These are secluded locations where the pups stay while the pack hunts. Here the pups practice their hunting skills on mice, small mammals and insects such as bumblebees and grasshoppers. The pack might choose several such sites during the summer. By fall, the pups are ready to hunt with the pack; now all travel together and go much farther afield.

The Pack

The basic unit of wolf society is the pack. It consists of about six to twelve animals, but can vary in size from two to the high teens. It is made up of a dominant male called the alpha male (who is usually the leader), a dominant female called the alpha female (who is sometimes the leader), and yearlings, pups and other mature wolves.

The alpha male and female are usually, but not always, the breeding pair. The alpha female viciously prohibits other females in the pack from breeding with the alpha male. The alpha male will also try to prevent any other males from breeding with the alpha female when she is in heat.

Pups are part of the pack and the pack as a group is involved in their protection, feeding and care. By the fall of their first year the pups hunt with the pack. After one year they are indistinguishable from adults.

The pack order is maintained by a "pecking order" or class system. The dominant male is the leader; he leads on hunts, makes decisions and takes on responsibilities. He expects submissive behaviour from all other wolves in the pack. If they do not give this spontaneously, he will demand it by aggressive snarls, mounting, or, if necessary, fighting.

The next most dominant wolf, the beta male, extracts the same obedience and submissiveness from those below him, and so on down to the last wolf who is picked on by all.

Lone wolves make up about 15 percent of the wolf population. They can be young that have moved away when the pack size has become too large, or low-order wolves that have been expelled from the pack.

Pack cohesiveness is reinforced by group feeding, group hunting, group sleeping and group ritual. Before a hunt the wolves gather,

touch noses and wag tails. This seems to bind them as a team. They rub and touch the leader when he wakes up or returns to the group. Again, this seems to reinforce the closeness of the pack.

Group howling is likely the best known pack activity. Not only does it serve to identify and locate individuals, it also keeps them in touch with the rest of the pack and serves to warn other packs of their presence. It seems to have a therapeutic effect as well—the wolf's equivalent of Saturday night discos or Sunday morning spirituals.

The Hunt

Most animals that prey on animals larger than themselves usually hunt in packs as do wolves. Wolves sometimes follow or track their prey but always chase them in the end. They have great speed and can maintain it for some time. However, if prey is escaping, wolves usually give up the chase quite quickly.

Wolves often choose vulnerable individuals first: the old, young, sick or wounded. Wolves generally attack the rump of the animal. Severe wounds weaken the animal, slowing it down until the wolves complete the kill. Wolves usually eat the animal in one or two days. Occasionally they store it, and sometimes they do not eat it at all. Wolves eat rapidly and can consume large quantities of meat at a sitting.

After a successful hunt the wolves gorge, rest and then move on to hunt again. Frequently they travel as far as 40 km (25 miles) before they make another kill. The hunts are often unsuccessful. It is estimated that wolves make a kill about every five days in winter—a true feast or famine existence.

Wolves and ravens are often seen together. The wolves provide free bone pickings for the ravens, and the ravens locate dead and dying animals for the wolves. The wolves and the ravens can follow each other to potential meals. Such a relationship where both benefit is called "symbiotic."

Foxes too benefit from wolf kills and often move in when the wolves have had their first fill. Wolves and foxes get along much like cats and dogs: wolves sometimes tolerate foxes and at other times chase or even kill them.

Wolves and People

In general, wolves avoid all contact with humans. Most of us will never see one. There are no documented reports of unprovoked wolf attacks in North America. If a wolf has rabies—a terrible disease that may drive an animal to become aggressive towards people—it may attack. At present, rabies is not a problem in wolves, but outbreaks can occur.

People and wolves sometimes compete for the same food. This has brought people and wolves into conflict over the years. Wolves will sometimes kill or maul domestic livestock. These are often attacks on unprotected calves or yearlings.

The main prey of wolves are the same species pursued by big game hunters. This has brought people and wolves into competition and has sometimes resulted in wolf control when large wild game populations decline.

People have shot, trapped and poisoned wolves. As a result, most wolves are now restricted to the wilder areas of the North and mountain parks, where they have established a healthy breeding population.

Wolf Language

"If you come one step closer you're going to get it!"

"OK! OK! I give up"

"Let's Play!"

Coyotes

Description

The **coyote**, **brush wolf** or **prairie wolf** (*Canis latrans*), looks like a collie-sized dog. It is a small wolf, about half the size of its larger relative. The coyote has a long, fox-like muzzle, quite large pointed ears, thinner legs than a dog's, small feet and a bushy tail, usually with a black tip. Coyotes living in mountain and forested areas are a darker colour than those living on the prairies. Their colour helps them blend with their surroundings. Their average weight is 13 kg (28 lbs.). The male is slightly bigger than the female.

Location

The coyote is found throughout the West. Because of its adaptability it is one of the few mammals that has been able to increase its range and tolerate humans.

Food

Coyotes eat just about anything. Their varied menu includes rabbits, hares, squirrels, beaver, voles, mice, birds and insects, the latter a favourite with the pups. Coyotes prey on the unprotected young of larger mammals, such as deer and antelope. Even some of the weaker adults become a tasty meal for coyotes.

Coyotes also dine on food that does not run away: such as berries, fruits and dead animals or "carrion". A large percentage of the coyote's winter diet is carrion. Coyotes compete with foxes, badgers, lynx, bobcats and other small predators for food.

Predators

Wolves, cougars, great horned owls and golden eagles prey on coyotes, especially the pups.

Reproduction

Females usually start breeding at two years, although some start at a year. Mating most often occurs in February, when the females come into heat. Gestation is about 60 to 63 days. Usually five to seven pups—sometimes 12 or more—are born in early April. Coyotes have one litter each year. Pairs tend to stay together for several years.

Hunting for food is a coyote's main activity. The coyote must practice its hunting techniques over and over if it is to catch something to eat. This training starts early with the pups practicing their pouncing on insects.

Coyotes have good senses of smell and hearing. They can hear mice squeak in runways under the snow, even if the snow is very deep. The coyote "freezes," then pounces on the mouse when it emerges.

Coyotes can pick up a person's scent from 1.5 km (a mile) or more away.

The coyote has been called clever and its association with the badger is proof of the coyote's legendary hunting skills. While badgers dig out the holes of ground squirrels, coyotes sometimes wait nearby for the ground squirrels, who are trying to escape the badgers.

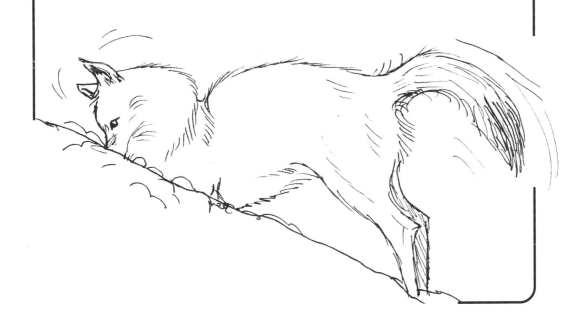

Teamwork is an important part of the coyote's hunting technique.

When chasing jack rabbits (prairie hares), which run faster than coyotes but tend to go in a circular pattern, a pair of coyotes form a relay team. One coyote relieves the other as it tires, giving each a chance to rest while waiting for the jack rabbit to come around again.

Another form of cooperative hunting occurs when one coyote waits by the home of a prey while another chases the prey home.

Coyotes catch the young of large mammals, such as pronghorn, by teamwork. One coyote will distract the larger pronghorn (usually the mother) while the second coyote comes in and carries off the defenseless young.

Coyotes hunt singly and in pairs, and also in groups called "clans." Coyotes prey on deer during harsh winters, when the deer are exhausted from breaking through deep, crusted snow and weak from lack of food.

Family Life

The female digs several dens before she gives birth. If danger threatens, the male and female move the pups to a safer den. The pups are moved quite frequently, especially when there is a heavy infestation of fleas. The dens are kept very clean and are not smelly.

When the female coyote is nursing the pups in the first few days after birth, the male brings her food.

Calls

Coyotes are social animals, though not as sociable as wolves. They have a communication system that consists of scent markings and different calls. The calls let other coyotes know that an area is occupied. This discourages competition from other coyotes.

The higher the number of coyotes in an area the less food is available for any particular animal. This lowers the average litter size. The number of coyotes in a forested area varies with food availability, particularly if the main food source is a fluctuating population of snowshoe hares.

A trip into the country, day or night, is a delight to listeners if they are fortunate enough to hear the howl of coyotes. Even the pups join in as the adult coyotes begin their wailing. The coyote howl usually starts with a long, high-pitched howl and ends in a group of sharp yips and yaps.

When a few coyotes are giving their singsong it sounds like there are many more coyotes around. There are about 11 different calls which apparently have meaning to the coyote.

The coyote has been called "God's dog" by the Indians, who have recognized its ability to survive and its willingness to make the most of a situation. To have coyote-like abilities, such as cleverness, was held in high esteem by Indians. Many Indian legends have Coyote as the Creator or as Trickster, a powerful teacher.

Other people, especially sheep ranchers, have seen the coyote as a competitor, a robber of livestock. In spite of people's attempt to exterminate the coyote, it has extended its range, unlike the wolf whose range and numbers have been reduced by its inability to cope with people's control measures.

An early prairie shelter dug in the ground was called a "coyote house."

Red Fox

Description

The **red fox** (*Vulpes vulpes*) is about half the size of a coyote. It has a bushy coat, mainly reddish-brown.

There are three other colour variations: **black**, **silver** (black with silver tips), and **cross**, all of which sometimes lend their name to this species. The cross marking—a dark cross on the back and shoulders of a red fox—is unusual. All colour variations can occur in the same litter.

Foxes' ears are large and perky. They have keen noses and sharp eyes. The red fox has a long, fluffy tail with a white tip. Their tails are as long as their bodies. Their legs have dark "stockings." The southern red fox is slightly smaller and paler than the northern red fox.

Location

The red fox is distributed throughout Canada and the US. It is very adaptable and clever. It can move to where food is found and may live close to human habitation. Coyotes and foxes compete for the same food. Foxes need to use all their skill and intelligence to avoid coyotes.

Food

Foxes are great mousers. They also eat hares and rabbits, plants, berries, birds, birds' eggs, insects and carrion. They are definitely omnivores.

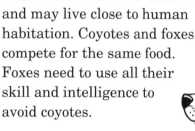

Predators

Foxes are preyed upon by coyotes, lynx and eagles.

Reproduction

Foxes are monogamous (they have only one mate in a breeding season). Mating generally takes place in March. After a gestation period of about 50 days, two to seven pups are born in late April. They are ready to leave the den when they are about a month old, and they play like puppies until they are skilled and big enough to be on their own. Red foxes often live in dens in the forest where there is good cover. Rather than dig their own dens, they usually prefer to inhabit woodpiles, brush piles or abandoned woodchuck or badger burrows.

Neat Notes

Red foxes are very fast and secretive, and they are out and about at twilight and night. Since they occur where wolves are found, they must be clever at avoiding confrontations. They will eat leftovers from wolf kills.

The female fox is called a "vixen," the male, a "dog fox." The young are called "pups."

Foxes bark.

Foxes have fur between their toes which help to keep their feet warm in winter. Their bushy tails can be wrapped around their faces while sleeping to keep their noses warm.

Northern populations of red foxes rise and fall with the population of snowshoe hares, which are their main food source.

145

Swift Fox

Description

The **swift fox** (*Vulpes velox*) is about the size of a large house cat. It is yellowish-grey and has a greyish tail with a black tip. The swift fox is curious and trusting. It has a sweet face with small ears.

Location

The swift fox is found on the prairies.

Food

It eats mice, rabbits, hares, ground squirrels, insects, birds, birds' eggs, berries, plants and carrion.

Predators

Coyotes, eagles and great horned owls eat the swift fox.

Reproduction

Similar to the red fox, which is described above.

Neat Notes

The swift fox is very swift! "Swift fox" rather than "kit fox" is the correct name of this prairie mammal. The kit fox is its desert cousin.

Like the red fox, the swift fox is most active at night. They use their dens all year, unlike other members of the dog family.

The swift fox, once abundant, is now rare. Much of their habitat disappeared when cropland replaced native prairie. They were also trapped, and many succumbed to poison baits that were set out for coyotes. In 1983, they were reintroduced to the Canadian prairies and appear to be making a comeback. Good luck to them!

The **gray fox** (*Urocyon cinereoargenteus*) can be found in south-eastern Manitoba, the Dakotas and Wyoming. It can climb trees.

Poems, Songs & Stories

Sly is the Word

Some people are busy—
As busy as bees—
And others are quiet as mice;
Or eager as beavers,
Or crazy as loons,
Or happy as larks—which is nice.
Some people are stubborn—
As stubborn as mules—
And others are dumb as an ox;
But never was anyone,
Anywhere, anytime
Nearly as sly as a fox.

by Richard Shaw
from *The Fox Book*

Traditional
from *Songs to Grow On*

The Fox

The fox went out on a star-lit night,
He prayed the moon for to give him light,
For he'd many a mile to go that night,
Before he reached the town-O.
Town-O, town-O
For he'd many a mile to go that night;
Before he reached the town-O.

At last he came to a farmer's yard,
The ducks and the geese were mighty scared,
"The best of you shall grease my beard,
"Before I leave the town-O,
"Town-O, town-O,
"The best of you shall grease my beard,
"Before I leave the town-O."

He grabbed the grey goose by the neck,
He threw a duck across his back,
And he heeded not their "quack, quack, quack,"
The legs all dangling down-O....

Old Mother Slipper-Slopper jumped out-a bed,
And out the window pop't her head
Crying "John, John, the grey goose is dead,
"The fox is on the town-O...."

Then John ran up to the top of the hill,
And blew his horn both loud and shrill.
"Blow on," said the fox, "your music still,
"While I trot home to my den-O...."

At last he came to his cozy den,
Where sat his young ones, nine or ten,
They said, "Daddy, you must go there again,
For it sure is a lucky town-O...."

The fox and wife without any strife,
They cut up the goose with fork and knife,
And said 'twas the best they had eat in their life,
And the young ones picked the bones-O....

How Coyote Stole Fire

North American Indians traditionally respect animals and believe that they have strong spirits. The coyote's cleverness make him highly revered by Natives.

A long time ago when moms and dads first came to the world they were happy almost all the time. They were happy with the spring that brought new life to the land. They were happy with the summer that helped the flowers and the children grow. And they were happy with the autumn that brought colourful leaves and tasty berries for the children to collect. But, they were sad with winter as it brought cold and hunger and sometimes a great loss. They wished that they could take a bit of the sun and bring it to their village so they could have warmth during the winter.

One spring, as Coyote was passing by the village, he heard their sad cry and felt sorry for the furless moms, dads and children, who had been so cold during the winter. His fur had given him warmth during the winter. Suddenly Coyote remembered where there was fire. Far away on a mountain top three Fire Beings kept guard over a fire. But they were very selfish and didn't want to share their fire with anyone.

Coyote decided to go there and bring some of the fire back to the village. He climbed to the top of the mountain and sat in the bushes watching the three Fire Beings. The Fire Beings had glowing eyes and big claws on their hands. Coyote watched them all day and all night and discovered that there was a time just before sunrise when one of the Fire Beings had a hard time rising from his sleep to take his turn at guarding the fire.

Coyote made a plan and went to talk about it with some of the other animals. He then climbed back up the mountain and watched the Fire Beings, all day and all night. Then, just as the lazy Fire Being was about to get up and watch the fire, Coyote grabbed a piece of the fire and ran down the mountain.

The Fire Beings chased after him and one of them managed to grab Coyote by the tail leaving a black mark which you can even see today. Now Coyote yelled and threw the fire to Squirrel who caught it and put it on his back and ran through the tree tops. The fire was very hot on Squirrel's back so she curled her tail over her back just like she does now. Squirrel then threw the fire to Chipmunk. Chipmunk, a little scared, waited and then ran just as one of the Fire Beings came close. The Fire Being managed to run three of its claws down Chipmunk's back leaving three marks which can be seen even today. Chipmunk threw the fire to Frog and Frog tried to leap away but one Fire Being grabbed him by the tail and all seemed lost. But Frog pulled with all his might and broke away from his tail which he never got again.

Frog threw the fire to Wood and Wood swallowed it. The Fire Being went to Wood and tried to shake the fire out of him but Wood kept fire inside of him. Finally, the Fire Beings gave up and went back to their mountain top. Coyote, being the smart animal person that he was, knew how to get fire out of Wood. He went back to the village and showed the moms and dads and children how to rub two dry sticks together to get the fire out. From then on the village had warmth in winter.

a Crow Indian legend
from *Coyote the Trickster*

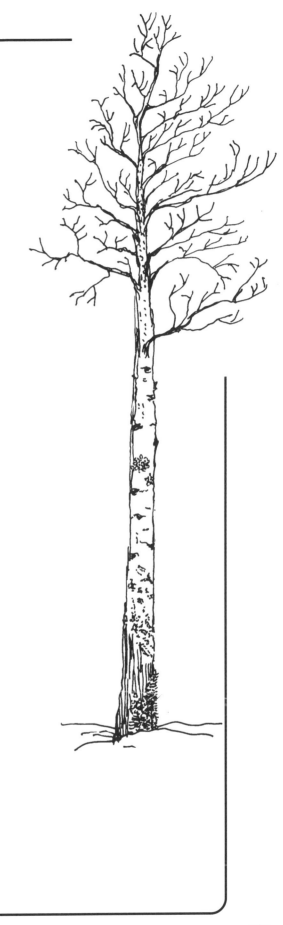

Coyotes

The coyotes are howling;
it's forty below.
The moon is silvering
shivering snow.

Keeipipipipiipipipipipip

kaiueoo ooo oo

eeee ya ya ya ya ya yup

oooooooooooooooooooooooooooooooooooooooooooooooooo o o o o o o o o o o o

pukaaaaaa

apapapapapap

keeoohahahahahahaahaahaa kyip

The coyotes are crying;
the night is awake
with their crying at midnight
on the frozen lake.

aueeeeoooo ooouiiiiui wa wa wa wa wa a i wa a i wa a i a ii a ii a i

yute yieeyeet yite

eaeeeeeeeeeeeeeeeeeee e e e e e e

Hark to the barking
low notes and wry notes,
the barking bravado,
the kai-yi-yipping
and kai-yi-yapping
of coy-yi coy-otes.

by Jon Whyte
from *Prairie Jungle*

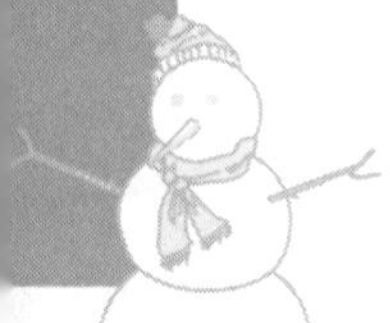

Pierre and the Wolf
(a modern fable)

Pierre was a little boy who lived in the Swan Hills of Alberta. His dad was a trapper, a hunter and a guide. His mom cooked, made their clothes, worked in their garden, tanned the furs, attended meetings, took care of people when they were hurt or sick, was a member of council, taught school to Pierre and his brothers and sisters and loved them very, very much.

Pierre had a small trap line. One day he left home early. There was not much food at home; the hunting had been very bad.

At the first trap, he found a hare. As he was releasing the trap a big wolf came up and said, "I'm hungry."

Pierre was surprised. Wolves don't talk.

"Well, I'm hungry too," Pierre replied, and put the hare in his sack.

The wolf took a step closer. Pierre handed over the hare.

At the next stop Pierre found a nice fat beaver in the trap.

"Great," he thought, "meat to eat and a pelt to sell."

He pulled the beaver up and was putting it in his sack when he heard a sound behind him.

"Excuse me" a too-familiar voice said, "but I'm very hungry and I would like that beaver."

"Well, my brothers and sisters and I are very hungry too," Pierre replied, and put the beaver in his sack. The wolf, who had decided Pierre was a better hunter than she, had followed him from the last stop. She was really very hungry, so she bared her teeth, raised her tail and raised the hair on her neck, and Pierre handed over the beaver.

Pierre was getting discouraged. The wolf was now trailing after him and Pierre knew what would happen when he reached his next trap.

Just then Pierre spotted an old, lone moose.

"Oh, if I were a little older and could use the rifle, I could get food for the whole family," he thought. Then he thought again and had to hide his smile from the wolf.

The wolf had seen the moose too. Feeling better with a hare and beaver in her tummy, she set out after the moose. Pierre waited patiently. Soon the wolf had captured the moose. Pierre approached.

"I'm hungry," said Pierre.

The wolf looked up. "I'm hungry too."

"But you have already had a hare and a beaver."

"But I need food for my pups," said the wolf.

Then Pierre pulled himself up tall, bared his teeth, raised his arms, and made as big a noise as he could: "AARARARARRAR."

The wolf jumped back in surprise.

Pierre put a rope around the legs of the moose and dragged that moose all the way home. His mother and father and sisters and brothers saw him coming and cheered. What a feast they had!

That night, Pierre tiptoed out of bed, pulled on his parka and went to the storehouse. He took the saw and cut off a big hunk of meat. He went outside, and, looking around, saw two glinting eyes at the edge of the clearing. He threw the meat as hard as he could.

And in the Swan Hills that night, the families of both Pierre and the wolf went to bed with full tummies.

by Dianne Hayley

Follow-Up Activities

Coyote Round-Up

For a group of six or more children and two leaders.

Designate a "home" for the squirrels and another area a distance away as a feeding area. Food can be coloured paper, fabric scraps, foam packing chips or other such visible objects.

One of the leaders should be the coyote. The children will be squirrels.

The object of the game is for the squirrels to leave home, get a piece of food and return safely without being caught by the coyote.

The coyote hides behind a tree. When he is ready he makes a "yip" noise.

Squirrels become coyotes when they are caught.

Before all the squirrels get eaten, begin another adventure or wait until all squirrels are eaten and play again.

What's That Sound?

Coyotes have sharp senses—especially hearing and smelling. The following two activities are fun and help the children practice their own hearing skills. The children sit in a circle with their eyes closed and listen for sounds that a leader makes (or use taped sounds). The children try to guess the sounds.

A variation of this game is to have the children sit in a circle and again close their eyes. Have them pretend that they are coyotes listening for mice. The leader picks one or two children to go and hide somewhere in the room. The leader encourages the children to keep their eyes closed and listen for sounds. The children who are hiding make little squeaking sounds. Whoever points first to where the sound is coming from can be the next to hide. This game can also be played outside.

What Time Is It Mr. Wolf?

The leader begins as the wolf. The children line up side by side. They say, "What time is it Mr. Wolf?" If the wolf replies, "five o'clock," they take five steps toward him, and so on. The game continues until the wolf replies "Dinner time!" Then all children run back to the starting line. Anyone caught by the wolf becomes the wolf for the next game.

Fox and Geese

Have the children follow the leader and tramp a large circle in fresh snow. Tramp paths through the centre as if cutting a pie. Geese and foxes can only travel on these lines. The centre is safety, home free, where the geese are safe from the fox.

One child is the fox and chases the geese. When a goose is touched, he or she becomes the fox and the fox becomes a goose. The fox cannot be tagged back immediately. Adjust to the age of the group.

Tracking

Look for tracks in new or wet snow. This is a super way to find out who is living in your neighbourhood. It is fun to track your Mom, Dad and friends since our boot prints are very distinctive. Check in the other sections of this book for the footprints of other animals.

Animal Tracks to Keep

Materials: plaster of Paris
water
large milk carton
petroleum jelly (optional)
spoon for mixing

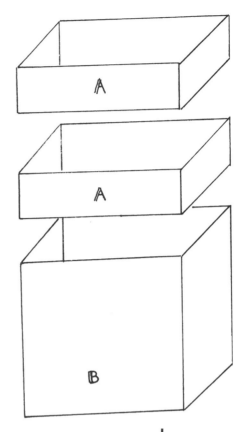

Cut the milk carton 10 cm (4") from the bottom to make a mixing bowl. Then cut two rims (A) at least five cm (2") high from the remainder of the carton.

Find a nice, deep track.

Put one rim around the track, pushing it into the ground slightly.

Mix the plaster of Paris and water to the consistency of a milk shake.

Pour into the mold. Wait about 20 minutes. You can poke a hole in the cast just before it hardens so it can be hung on a wall. Remove the cast carefully. This will give you a negative impression of the track.

For a positive mold, grease this first mold well with petroleum jelly, and also grease the second rim. Put the rim on the ground, press in. Half fill rim with a new mixture of plaster of Paris, then press the negative mold firmly on top and wait 20 minutes. Pull apart carefully.

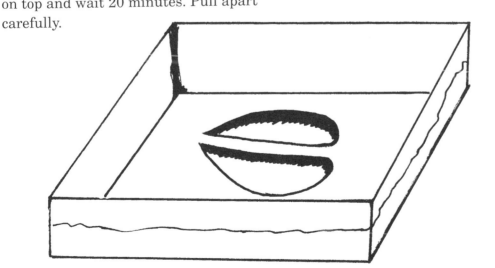

Coyote Finger Puppet

Materials:

    felt scraps: grey or tawny for body;
       black for nose, whiskers and pupils;
       white for eyes
    scissors
    needle and thread, or glue

Cut out puppet using diagram as a pattern. Sew or glue together. Add eyes, nose and whiskers.

Shadow Wolf Puppet

Place your hand in the beam of a strong light to produce a shadow.

The thumb becomes the lower jaw of the wolf. The fingers become its upper jaw. The knuckles of the hand become the crown of the wolf's head.

You can now pretend the wolf is eating or talking by opening and closing the thumb and fingers.

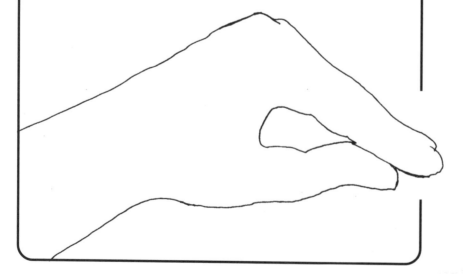

Winter Nights

Winter Nights

Nights last longer during winter than at any other time time of the year, and there are more bright stars visible in the sky. Winter is a wonderful time to get to know some of these stars, so choose a clear night, dress warmly and take the whole family out to stare at the sky. Bring along a lawn chair and a cozy quilt. If you live in the city, find an area that is away from the bright street lights. Sometimes your backyard is not dark enough, so you may have to find a park or schoolyard. Those who live in the country, where the air is clearer and the sky is darker, can see many more stars than those in the city.

Watch for other things that move in the sky such as airplanes, man-made satellites and meteorites.

The Moon

The largest bright object in the night sky is the **moon**. The moon is Earth's only natural satellite. The moon is a large round ball of rock and it does not have water or air. It only shines because it reflects the light from the sun just like the reflector on a bicycle.

Only one side of the moon can be seen from Earth. As the moon travels around Earth, taking 29.5 days to do so, different parts of the moon are lit by the sun. The different parts that we see from Earth are called "phases of the moon."

When the moon is on the side of the earth that is near the sun, the side lit by the sun faces away from us and we can hardly see the moon—that is called the "new moon."

When the moon travels to the opposite side of the earth from the sun the side we see is all lit. We call that a "full moon."

When you look at this very simplified drawing, remember to put yourself at the X and look out at the moon as it moves around the earth.

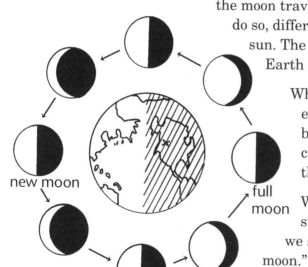

SUN

new moon

full moon

Look at a calendar for the dates of the different phases and see for yourself if the moon is in the same phase as stated by the calendar.

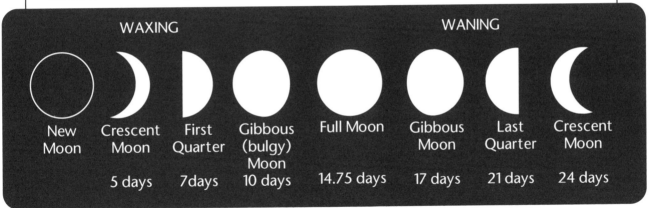

WAXING				WANING			
New Moon	Crescent Moon	First Quarter	Gibbous (bulgy) Moon	Full Moon	Gibbous Moon	Last Quarter	Crescent Moon
	5 days	7 days	10 days	14.75 days	17 days	21 days	24 days

Neat Notes The moon has been a source of wonder and mystery for thousands of years. For most of that time, no one thought we earthlings could build a spaceship that would take a man 384,400 km (238,900 miles) to the moon. The Apollo astronauts, Neil Armstrong and Edwin Aldrin were the first humans to step onto the surface of the moon on July 20, 1969.

Stars

As we stare at the dark sky we can see thousands of points of light. Some are bright; some are faint. These points of light are **stars**, which are extremely hot, glowing balls of gas. Except for the sun, which is the nearest star to Earth, stars are trillions of kilometres or miles away, or more. The sun is less than 150 million kilometres (about 93 million miles) away.

Our view of the stars changes with the seasons. People have named some of the shapes they see in the stars, like connect-the-dots pictures. We call these named groups of stars "constellations."

Stars do not twinkle out in space, but when the light from a star hits the air around the earth, the air changes the path of the light and the stars seem to twinkle.

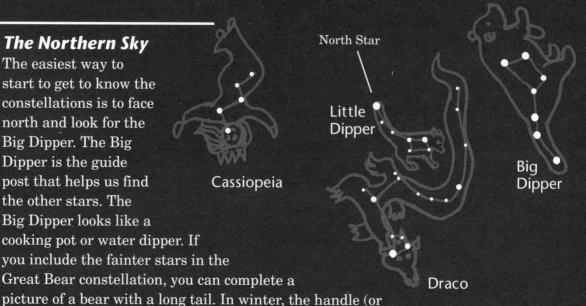

North Star

Little Dipper

Cassiopeia

Draco

Big Dipper

The Northern Sky

The easiest way to start to get to know the constellations is to face north and look for the Big Dipper. The Big Dipper is the guide post that helps us find the other stars. The Big Dipper looks like a cooking pot or water dipper. If you include the fainter stars in the Great Bear constellation, you can complete a picture of a bear with a long tail. In winter, the handle (or tail) of the Big Dipper hangs down towards the horizon.

The two bright stars in the Big Dipper, farthest from the handle are called the "pointer stars." They point the way to the North Star. Follow a line through these stars, five times as long as the distance between the pointer stars to a medium bright star, the North Star.

The North Star is also called Polaris or the Pole Star. This star showed sailors which way was north. It is also the end star in the handle of the Little Dipper.

The Little Dipper looks like smaller version of the Big Dipper and is known also as the Little Bear or Ursa Minor. Except for the North Star, its stars are so faint they are often lost in the glow of city lights. Draco (pronounced DRAY-ko) the Dragon curves its way between the Big Dipper and the Little Dipper, but most of its stars are faint and hard to see.

Using the Big Dipper as our guide post, again draw an imaginary line from the second star on the Dipper's handle, through the North Star to the constellation Cassiopeia, which is shaped like a "W." Cassiopeia, according to Greek legend, is the queen who sits in a chair.

These stars in the north sky are dependable and can be seen at any time of the year on a clear night. Watch for them this winter, and again next summer to see if their positions have changed.